D0045169

THE CLUE OF THE WHISTLING BAGPIPES

WARNINGS not to go to Scotland can't stop Nancy Drew from setting out on a thrill-packed mystery adventure.

Undaunted by the vicious threats, the attractive young detective—with her father and her two close friends—goes to visit her great-grandmother at an imposing estate in the Scottish Highlands, and to solve the mystery of a missing family heirloom.

And there is another mystery to be solved: the fate of flocks of stolen sheep.

Baffling clues challenge Nancy's powers of deduction: a note written in the ancient Gaelic language, a deserted houseboat on Loch Lomond, a sinister red-bearded stranger in Edinburgh, eerie whistling noises in the Highlands. Startling discoveries in an old castle and in the ruins of a prehistoric fortress, on a rugged mountain slope and in a secluded glen, lead Nancy closer to finding the solutions to both mysteries.

Wearing a time-honored tartan, Nancy climbs the mountain of Ben Nevis in the dark of night and plays a tune of historic heroism on the bagpipes—all part of her daring plan to trap the sheep thieves and to recover the valuable family heirloom.

"The piper must be signaling!"

NANCY DREW MYSTERY STORIES

The Clue of the
Whistling Bagpipes

BY CAROLYN KEENE

NEW YORK

Grosset & Dunlap

PUBLISHERS

© BY GROSSET & DUNLAP, INC., 1964

ALL RIGHTS RESERVED

ISBN: 0-448-09541-6

PRINTED IN THE UNITED STATES OF AMERICA

Contents

CHAPTER I

Mysterious Heirloom

"NANCY, lass, would ye fly off wi' me to the land o' bagpipes and kilts?" Mr. Drew asked her with a grin. "And how do you like my Scottish accent?'" he teased.

His daughter burst into laughter. "It's ver-r-ry good!" Nancy replied. "And will I be wearin' a kilt and dancin' to the pipes?" she countered, trying to imitate her father.

"You'll be solving a mystery," Mr. Drew answered in his natural voice. "The mystery of a missing heirloom—an heirloom of great value which was supposed to come to you, but has been mislaid or lost."

Nancy's eyes opened wide with interest. "It's for me? And it's in Scotland?"

Mr. Drew, a lawyer, explained that Nancy's maternal great-grandmother, Lady Douglas, who lived in Inverness-shire, had recently written to him. She intended to turn over her large house and estate to the National Trust of Scotland. This had been founded to preserve old castles, ruins, and other places of historic interest.

"In the case of the Douglas property, the transfer cannot be made until a number of relatives have signed releases," Mr. Drew went on. "Lady Douglas has asked me to get these signatures and also donations for an endowment from interested members of the Douglas family in the United States. In order to do this, I must go to Scotland and find out more about the case."

"The heirloom—" Nancy began, but was interrupted by the ringing of the telephone. "Excuse me, Dad. I'll see who it is."

The caller was Ned Nickerson, a college student who often dated Nancy. He had just returned from a trip to South America.

"I want to come over and tell you about it," Ned said.

"Oh, have dinner with us," Nancy replied. "Ned, it's wonderful to hear from you!" She laughed. "This will be sort of hello and good-by. Guess what! I'm flying to Scotland!"

"That's great!" Ned answered, then said, "Well, I'll see you at seven."

Nancy returned to her father and told him about the call. "Now, please tell me more about my heirloom," she begged.

Mr. Drew smiled. "I don't know what the

heirloom is—your great-grandmother didn't say. She only mentioned that it was missing."

At once Nancy was intrigued. "Was it lost in the house?"

"Lady Douglas didn't give any further details."

Nancy looked into space for several moments. Finally she said, "Could it have been stolen?"

"I suppose so," her father replied. "Now, I'll tell you about the trip to Scotland. In the first place, I must confer with lawyers in Glasgow, then Edinburgh. After that, we'll go up to Douglas House."

"It sounds terribly exciting!" said Nancy. "And it will be such fun going on a trip with you and also solving a mystery." She grinned. "Especially since I'll be looking for something that I know hardly anything about. And Douglas House is probably very beautiful."

Mr. Drew agreed. "I have been to Douglas House only once, and everything *was* very handsome. I can understand why the National Trust will be happy to open it to the public as a place of historic interest."

The lawyer said he would like to do a little work before dinner, so he went into his first-floor study. Nancy entered the kitchen, where the Drews' pleasant-faced housekeeper, Hannah Gruen, was just taking a lemon meringue pie from the oven.

"That looks luscious!" Nancy remarked.

Hannah Gruen had been mother and counselor to Nancy ever since the time she was a very young child, when her own mother had passed away.

The housekeeper looked fondly at Nancy. She was proud of the slender, attractive, titian-haired girl whose penchant for solving mysteries had brought fame and respect to the Drew household. From *The Secret of the Old Clock* to the revelations in *The Moonstone Castle Mystery,* Nancy had spent a great deal of her later teen-age years helping people uncover mysteries which were troubling them.

For the next hour, Nancy and Hannah Gruen talked about the proposed trip to Scotland and what clothing the girl should take. Nancy recalled to Hannah the almost unbelievable, fairy-like tales about her great-grandmother's life as the wife of a member of the House of Lords.

"To think that I'm going to see her at last!"

Hannah Gruen smiled. "I hope that heirloom is something small. This house is so full of trophies and objects from all over the world there isn't a corner left for another one!"

"Maybe we'll even have to move the piano out!" Nancy teased.

Just then the front doorbell rang and Nancy went to answer it. Ned Nickerson stood there, a wide grin on his handsome face. Nancy thought that next to her good-looking, athletic father, this special friend of hers was the nicest man she knew. He stood high in his classes at Emerson College, played football, and recently had been sent on a special assignment to South America in connection with his courses.

"Hi!" he said. "I left my car right back of yours on the street. Okay? Would you like me to put yours in the garage?"

"After a while, yes," Nancy answered. "But first, come and tell me all about yourself."

When they were seated in the living room, and Ned had described some of his exciting trips into the jungles, he remarked, "Nancy, in case you get lonesome in Scotland and want a mystery to solve, I can tell you about one."

Nancy's blue eyes sparkled. "What is it?"

Ned said that he had recently read in a newspaper about a ring of thieves who were stealing sheep and lambs in the Highlands of Scotland. "The authorities are baffled, so here's your chance, Nancy. You may as well solve the case of the poor gimmers!"

"The *what?*" Nancy asked.

"A gimmer is a young female lamb. Incidentally, how long will you be away, Nancy?"

"Dad didn't say. In fact, I doubt that he knows himself."

Ned gave a great sigh. "I'll have to talk to your father about getting you back here by June tenth.

My fraternity is giving a big windup party for the season," he announced. "You just have to be there."

"I ought to be able to make it," Nancy replied. "It's now the middle of May." She smiled broadly. "I'll do what I can to speed up my sleuthing."

"Good!" From a pocket Ned took out a small package and handed it to Nancy. "A souvenir from South America," he said.

The gift was a very unusual pin made of wood carved to represent a laughing monkey.

"He's adorable!" Nancy said, as she pinned the monkey on her blouse. "Thanks a million, Ned."

"The natives say it will bring good luck to the wearer," Ned informed her.

"Well, that's what I'll need if I expect to solve two mysteries in Scotland," Nancy told him, and explained about the missing heirloom.

Later, as they were finishing dinner, the telephone rang. Nancy excused herself to answer it. An excited girl's voice came over the wire. "Oh, Nancy, you've helped me win the most wonderful prize!"

"Bess Marvin," Nancy said to her blond, slightly plump but very attractive friend, "what are you talking about?"

Bess did not answer the question directly. "It's for two and you have to share it with me!"

"I? How? What is *it?*" Nancy exclaimed.

"It's so utterly marvelous I know you won't object. Nancy, this is what I did. I read about a contest offered by the magazine *Photographie Internationale*. A photograph had to be submitted. I used a picture of you sleuthing."

"What!" Nancy exclaimed, utterly amazed. She begged for more information and a clearer explanation of what had happened.

"We won a trip!" Bess almost shouted over the wire.

"Bess, please—"

But Bess had to tell the story in her own way. "Nancy, do you remember the picture of you with a magnifying glass, looking at the footprints?"

"Yes. Is that the one you sent in?"

"It's a wonderful picture!" said Bess. "It won *first* prize! And the prize is a trip for two to anywhere I want to go. Since you helped me win it, I think you ought to go with me!"

By this time Nancy, overwhelmed by the news, had dropped into the chair alongside the telephone table. She detested publicity, and here she had suddenly and inadvertently been brought to the attention of the reading public!

Bess rattled on. "You'll be famous all over the world! Newspapers and magazines and just everything will be printing the story!"

Nancy actually felt weak. If she was going to do any sleuthing in Scotland, the last thing she wanted was to be recognized. "Maybe I'll have to go incognito," she thought.

After a prolonged silence, Bess asked worriedly, "Are you still there? Don't you like—"

Nancy was suddenly jerked out of her reverie by a terrific crash on the street outside the Drew home. "Bess, I'll have to call you back," she said and hung up quickly.

By this time Ned had reached the hall. He and Nancy dashed outdoors and down the driveway toward the street. A dismaying sight met their eyes. An old but heavy truck had rammed head on into Nancy's car. That, in turn, had smashed into Ned's automobile.

Nancy was heartsick. She was very fond of her blue convertible which had played a big part in helping her solve mysteries. At first glance it looked to be a total wreck.

Nevertheless, her thoughts turned at once to the unfortunate driver of the truck. As she and Ned ran at top speed toward the accident scene, she said worriedly, "Oh, I hope the man isn't badly injured!"

CHAPTER II

A Plaid Clue

WHEN Nancy and Ned reached the smashed-in cab of the old truck, both closed their eyes for a second before getting up enough courage to look at a sight they dreaded to see. A light on the Drew grounds illuminated the twisted wreckage enough for them to view it clearly.

An expression of amazement came over Ned's face. "No one's in the cab!" he exclaimed.

Instantly Nancy realized that the door had been forced open. Perhaps the driver had been thrown clear! She quickly searched the street and around the truck, but no one was in sight.

"Ned, did you see anyone running away?" Nancy asked. Ned shook his head.

The couple examined the wreckage further. It was evident that no one was wedged between the pieces of crumpled metal and upholstery.

"Nancy, how could anyone have been in a

smashup like this and not been injured?" Ned asked.

"I'm sure no one could have," Nancy replied. "It's my guess that the truck driver jumped out before the crash and ran away."

Ned set his jaw. "This could even have been done on purpose!" he exclaimed.

"But why?" Nancy asked. "Why would anyone want to wreck my car?"

Now that she knew there was no injured person involved, she too became angry. Her beautiful convertible was ruined! She turned aside so that Ned could not see she was biting her lips to fight back tears.

While she was regaining control of her emotions, Ned dashed to the rear of the truck. "No license plate!" he fumed. "This proves the crash was caused deliberately!"

"Maybe we can trace the person by the engine number," Nancy suggested. "I'll get a flashlight."

As Nancy started up the driveway, she met Hannah Gruen and her father. Mr. Drew carried a flashlight in his hand. A moment later neighbors began to arrive. Everyone was amazed to learn that apparently the truck had run itself into Nancy's car.

Meanwhile, Nancy and Ned were searching the wreckage for the engine number. Finally they found the place where it had been, but the figures

"Why would anyone want to wreck my car?"
Nancy asked

had been cleverly scratched so as to be illegible!

"Now we have proof this whole thing was done on purpose!" Nancy told her father. "What I can't understand is why."

The lawyer frowned. "What did the person hope to accomplish?" he asked. "Obviously, he wasn't trying to injure you or Ned. And you hadn't planned any particular trip in your car, nor were you using it on any mystery."

Hannah Gruen offered to notify the police, while the others continued their investigation. First, they looked at Ned's car. Fortunately, there was no damage other than broken headlights and two bent fenders.

Next, they began searching the truck for clues to the owner or driver. There was no name or initials, but Nancy remarked that the police laboratory would be able to detect any lettering which might have been painted over.

"Have you looked inside the truck?" Mr. Drew asked his daughter.

"Not yet," Nancy answered.

She climbed into the back and beamed the flashlight around. There was nothing on the floor or sides. The person or persons who had caused the crash had removed every kind of identification.

In a few minutes a police car and two wreckers arrived. Flashlight photographs were taken and a fingerprint expert went to work on the wheel and door handles. The man reported that too many people had handled them to make a positive identification of any one set of prints.

"We're getting nowhere!" Nancy whispered to her father and Ned.

Presently the officers came over and queried the Drews, asking who they suspected might have perpetrated the incident.

"We have no idea," the lawyer replied.

As soon as the wreckers had hauled off Nancy's car and the truck, Ned taped Mr. Drew's flashlight and one of Nancy's onto the front of his car.

"I'd better get to a garage and have new headlights put in," he said. Before leaving, he added cheerily, "Nancy, if the police don't solve this mystery right away, suppose I try my hand at it while you're in Scotland?"

"That's a good idea," she agreed.

"I'll call you tomorrow to see if the police have found out anything," Ned said. He drove off, and one by one the neighbors sauntered back to their homes.

The Drews and Hannah Gruen went into the house and sat down to discuss the whole affair. But suddenly Nancy jumped up. "Bess!" she exclaimed. "I forgot that I promised to phone her back!"

When the connection was made, Bess complained, "What happened to you? I've been waiting here for ages!"

When Nancy told her what had caused the delay, Bess burst out, "How perfectly dreadful! And what an awful person to do such a thing! Well, I certainly hope the police find him!"

"I do too," said Nancy. "But now, tell me more about this trip you won."

Bess revealed that the trip could be made to any place in Europe. By the time she finished speaking, Nancy had an idea.

"Why don't you take your cousin George? Then we three girls can go with my dad."

"Do you mean it?" Bess asked.

"Of course I mean it."

"Where is your father going, by the way?"

"To Scotland. There are two mysteries waiting to be solved. Wouldn't you and George like to help tackle them?"

Bess's cousin, George Fayne, had been invaluable to Nancy in her detective work. She was level-headed and very courageous. She liked her name George, and tried to live up to it by wearing boyish haircuts and plain-tailored clothes. She was dark-haired, slender, and athletic.

"I'll phone George right away and let you know," Bess offered.

Within ten minutes she called back excitedly. "Everything's arranged! When do we leave? And will your dad make the reservations?"

Nancy hurried to ask her father. "We'll start

three days from now," he told her. "I'm glad the girls are coming along."

When Nancy relayed the news, Bess gasped. "Three days! We'll make it, but my goodness what a rush! I'm glad we have our old passports."

Nancy soon said good night to her father and Hannah Gruen and went to her room to start her packing. When she finally went to bed, the weary girl drifted off to sleep immediately. She was awake early, and helped prepare a breakfast of fresh strawberries, bacon and eggs, and muffins.

Not long after Mr. Drew had left the house, the postman arrived with a handful of letters. One, which was printed and bore no return address, was for Nancy. Curious, she opened it quickly. As she read the note inside, she gave a gasp of amazement.

"Bad news, Nancy?" Mrs. Gruen asked.

"Yes, in a way. This is a threat!"

"Oh, my goodness!" the woman exclaimed, and took the letter. Aloud she read: " *'Your wrecked convertible is just the first of a series of accidents that will befall you and any car you ride in.'* " The note was unsigned.

Nancy, fingering the envelope, thought she felt something inside it. She reached in and drew out a tiny square of plaid cloth.

"It's a piece of Douglas tartan!" she cried out.

Hannah Gruen looked perturbed. "What does this all mean?" she asked worriedly.

Nancy was silent for several seconds. Finally she said, "My guess is that the writer of this note is warning me that the accident is connected with my trip to Scotland. I wonder if it could have anything to do with the missing heirloom. Hannah, maybe whoever wrote this message is the thief and he doesn't want me to try finding it."

"But this letter was postmarked here in River Heights!" the housekeeper objected.

Nancy's forehead wrinkled in deep thought. "Maybe the valuable heirloom was shipped to this country. Anyway, I'm going to turn the note over to the police."

Nancy went off to do this, then spent the rest of the day shopping and talking to the garage repairman and to an agent of her automobile insurance company. Nancy was thankful that the convertible could be repaired, although the job would take some time. So far, the police had uncovered nothing regarding the owner of the truck or the person who had caused the wreck.

That evening Nancy and Hannah decided to take their terrier, Togo, for a little run. Mr. Drew was working in his study.

Half an hour later Nancy, after a long sprint, said, "Togo, you have me out of breath! I think you've had enough fresh air for tonight. Home we go!"

With the peppy terrier pulling on the leash, Nancy and Mrs. Gruen hurried home. Just as they started up the driveway, they saw a figure slip furtively away from the front of the house and go off toward the rear of the property. At once Nancy and the dog went after him, but by the time they reached the backyard, the man had disappeared.

At last they returned to the housekeeper, who declared, "Whoever that person is, his business wasn't honest or he wouldn't have sneaked away."

"I agree," said Nancy. "Let's see if we can find any clues to his identity."

She put Togo in the house, then took a flashlight from a drawer in the hall table. Nancy began looking for footprints and found some faint dirty marks coming up the steps to the front porch. Another set led away. Before Nancy had a chance to try following them, Hannah cried out, "Something just started ticking in the mailbox!"

Nancy turned quickly and looked at the wrought-iron mailbox which was fastened to a hook alongside the front door. An expression of horror came over her face.

"It's a bomb!" she cried out.

CHAPTER III

Unwanted Publicity

As NANCY dashed forward to yank the mailbox from the hook, Hannah Gruen warned, "Don't touch it!"

"The ticking just started," Nancy replied quickly.

In a split second the box was in her hands. She flung it far out onto the lawn. Nancy and Hannah waited breathlessly. So far there had been only five ticks. Six—seven—eight—nine—

BOOM!

The explosion ripped the box apart, dug a deep hole in the ground, and scattered dirt, stones, and debris in all directions.

The noise brought Mr. Drew outside on the run. "What happened?" he asked.

By this time Hannah, her knees trembling, had dropped into a porch chair. As Nancy began to speak, the housekeeper rocked back and forth furiously.

"It's terrible!" she said weakly.

Nancy felt somewhat shaky herself, but assured her father they were unharmed.

Mr. Drew was greatly concerned. "You two might have been killed!" he cried out angrily. "The perpetrator of this crime must be found!"

The lawyer said he would phone the police. As he disappeared into the house, Nancy went to the lawn and examined the fragments caused by the explosion. Her sharp eyes soon detected fresh bits of paper with writing on them.

"That's funny," she thought. "We've already taken in today's mail. Surely the person who planted the bomb didn't leave a note."

Nancy gathered up all the paper scraps she could find and showed them to Hannah, still seated on the porch. "I wonder when this note was put into the mailbox. Have you any idea, Hannah?"

The housekeeper frowned. "Well, just before dinner tonight, the doorbell rang. When I went to answer, no one was there. Do you suppose the person who left the note rang the bell and then ran?"

"Possibly." More puzzled than ever, Nancy went into the house and spread the scraps of paper on the dining-room table. It took her a while to place the tiny fragments in their proper positions. Although parts of words were missing, she could clearly get the meaning of the message. It said:

Drew is going to bomb you!

Nancy stared at the warning. Who had sent it? "And who or whatever is Drew?" she asked herself.

Hannah and Mr. Drew walked in to say that two policemen had arrived and were making moulages of the prowler's footprints. Nancy showed them the message.

The housekeeper threw up her hands in dismay. "I'm glad you're both going to Scotland. It certainly isn't safe for you around here!"

Nancy and her father were forced to agree, but Nancy added, "Even if I have a mysterious man for an enemy, I think I have an unknown woman for a friend. This looks like a woman's handwriting."

"Yes, it does," said Mr. Drew. "However, your unknown enemy is very sly. Who knows where he may strike next?"

While they were talking the front doorbell rang. The caller was Chief McGinnis of the River Heights police force. He and the Drews had often cooperated on solving local mysteries.

The chief was ushered into the dining room. After greeting Nancy, the middle-aged, good-natured officer said, "I want to hear about this whole mystery. Start at the beginning, Nancy."

She did so, and ended by showing him the message on the table.

He whistled softly. "If you have a piece of cardboard and some glue, I'd like to paste this warning together and take it to headquarters."

Nancy produced glue and cardboard and together they accomplished the tedious job. By this time the policemen had completed their work outside the house and reported to the chief. The two men then said good night and left.

Nancy continued to study the handwriting on the strange note. She was sure that it held a good clue to the solution of the mystery. Procuring a piece of tracing paper, she copied the message.

Chief McGinnis laughed. "Is this a challenge?" he asked. "I hear you're leaving for Scotland in a couple of days. You'll have to hurry if you're going to beat me in finding the writer of this note!"

Nancy chuckled. "It will have to wait. I've already planned some sleuthing for tomorrow."

In the morning Nancy told her father she was going to inquire of various shopkeepers if they had seen any Scottish persons in town who were strangers to the community. "Such a person might have sent that piece of plaid."

"Good luck!" he called as Nancy left the house.

She went from place to place, putting her questions but receiving only negative responses.

"That plaid lead certainly didn't pay off," Nancy told herself as she started for home.

As she walked up the main street her eye was attracted to the window of a photographic shop. Staring straight at her was her own photograph!

Nancy hurried to the window. In the center of the display was a copy of *Photographie Internationale*. On the cover was the picture of Nancy sleuthing with a magnifying glass.

"It's pretty good," she thought. "But oh, how I wish Bess had won the trip some other way!"

Nancy was so intent upon the magazine that she did not notice she was slowly being surrounded by a throng of curious persons. As she turned to leave, a cheer went up and everyone began to clap. This attracted the attention of more people, who came hurrying from every direction.

"It's really you—Nancy Drew!" exclaimed a little girl in the crowd. "You're famous!"

"You're the girl detective!" cried another.

Suddenly a boy pushed his way through to Nancy and begged, "Please, miss, may I have your autograph?" The boy had big, blue pleading eyes. He was very shabbily dressed, and Nancy guessed that his family had little to spend on clothes. She smiled sympathetically and wrote her name on the piece of paper he held out.

"Oh, thank you!" The boy grinned and moved to the back of the crowd.

"I want one too!" said a little girl, running forward. "But I haven't any paper."

"Oh, that's all right, honey," said Nancy. She opened her handbag and took out a small notebook. After writing her name on one of the pages, she tore it out and handed the signature to the child.

This became the signal for a dozen children to push forward and ask for Nancy's autograph. She graciously obliged, but as several adults came up, the young sleuth shook her head.

"I'm sorry," she said politely. "I did it just for the children."

As she spoke, Nancy noticed that the shabbily dressed little boy was still at the rear of the crowd. To her annoyance, he was actually handing her autograph to a man, who in turn was giving the boy a dollar bill for it!

"Why, the idea!" Nancy thought. She called out to the man, "I said the autographs were only for the children. Please give that back!"

Instead of doing this, the man gave her a supercilious grin. "Thanks, babe," he shouted. "This will come in handy!"

He wheeled and hurried down the street. Nancy was furious. Instinct told her he was a person of whom to beware. She must get back that paper!

Pushing through the surprised crowd, she dashed down the street. Her quarry, who had had a good head start, turned a corner. When Nancy reached it, he was nowhere in sight. Disappointed, she retraced her steps and once more started up Main Street.

To her relief, the crowd at the photography shop had dispersed. The only one who lingered was the little boy who had sold her signature.

Seeing Nancy, he rushed to her side. "Please, may I have another autograph?" he asked.

Nancy was angry. Placing her hands on his shoulders, she faced him squarely. "To sell?" she asked.

The little boy began to quiver. "N-no," he stammered. "It's just for me."

"Who was that man you sold my autograph to?"

The boy began to cry. "I don't know—honest I don't. After you said you wouldn't give out autographs to grownups, he waved that dollar bill in my face and I couldn't say No. My mother needs money awful bad."

Nancy released her grip on the boy's shoulders. He kept insisting he was telling the truth. "All right," said Nancy finally, taking the note pad from her purse. "Suppose you give me *your* autograph, and write down your address too."

The lad gladly did so. Nancy took it and said, "Johnny Barto, some time I will come to your house, and if I find you *have* been telling the truth, I'll give you another autograph." She smiled and patted him on the shoulder. "All right?"

The boy smiled back, said he was sorry, and shuffled off. Nancy was tempted to follow him, still a bit suspicious that he did know who the purchaser of her signature was. Various thoughts flashed through her mind. Why was the man so eager to obtain the signature? Did he plan to use it in some illegal way?

She stood lost in thought until the boy had disappeared from view. "I do believe his story," she said to herself. "But perhaps I'll ask Ned to go to Johnny's house and check. I certainly miss having my own car to use!"

Nancy continued to reflect. "Anyway, I did get a good look at the man who bought my autograph. He was of medium height, thin, had a shock of black hair, and red cheeks."

Ideas about the man came to her quickly. Could he have planted the bomb? Had he caused the crash that had wrecked her car? Since she had had no success learning about any strange Scotsman, Nancy decided to change her tactics.

"I'll concentrate on trying to learn the identity of that man who bought my autograph!"

Her quest was unsuccessful until she came to a drugstore. It was owned by a Mr. Gregg, and the Drews frequently bought supplies there.

As Nancy walked up to the counter, Mr. Gregg, a stout, jolly person, said, "Hello, Nancy. Another mystery giving you a big headache? You'd like some aspirin?"

Nancy chuckled. "I have a mystery, but I don't need aspirin. I came for some information."

"Well, since you're a customer of long standing, I can give you information free," said the druggist with a grin.

Nancy described the man who had purchased her autograph, saying she would like to find out who he was. To her delight, Mr. Gregg said, "I guess I can help you a little."

The pharmacist told her that a man answering her description often came into the store to use the telephone. "I once heard somebody call him Pete, but I don't know his last name. Today he rushed in and made a beeline for the booth. Didn't close the door all the way. I happened to walk by just in time to hear him say 'Everything's jake. I got that girl's autograph.' "

Nancy was so pleased over the clue she felt like cheering. But she mercly expressed her appreciation and hurried from the drugstore.

The young detective went directly to police headquarters and told Chief McGinnis what had happened to her during the past hour and her suspicions regarding the man called Pete.

The chief listened attentively. "I'm glad you came, Nancy. I'll assign some of my men right away to the job of trying to locate this Pete. I

UNWANTED PUBLICITY 27

don't promise anything, though, before you leave for Scotland."

Nancy smiled. "The main thing is to catch him!" she said. "I'm convinced he's mixed up with these mysterious events. If you do find him, or get any leads, be sure to let me know!"

She wrote down the names of the hotels in Glasgow and Edinburgh where she would be staying, and finally Lady Douglas' address.

When Nancy reached home, Hannah told her that Ned had phoned. He wanted to come and say good-by to Nancy but would be busy all afternoon writing a report of his South American trip.

The housekeeper continued, "I took the liberty of inviting Ned to dinner. I thought you wouldn't mind," she added, winking.

Nancy gave the housekeeper a hug and went up to her own room to finish packing. There would be no chance that evening!

Ned arrived at six o'clock. "I hope you don't mind my coming early, Nance," he said. "I brought something to show you. I just couldn't wait any longer for your reaction."

He handed her the *Evening Graphic*. It was a sensational newspaper which normally would not have been purchased by Ned Nickerson or the Drews.

Nancy unfolded the paper and held it up. She

gave a cry of utter astonishment. On the front page, in bold type, was the caption:

Autograph Snatcher Enrages
Girl Detective!

Below was a large and not flattering candid snapshot of Nancy chasing the mysterious man!

CHAPTER IV

"Scots, Wha Hae"

As NANCY stared in dismay at the newspaper, Ned remarked, "I thought you were keeping your sleuthing trip to Scotland a secret."

"I *was* trying to!"

Ned pointed to the article. "This story tells everything—that you and your father are going to Scotland to solve the mystery of a lost heirloom which your great-grandmother planned to give you."

"But how in the world did the *Graphic* get the story?" Nancy asked, puzzled.

"What about Bess and George?" Ned suggested.

Nancy was sure that the cousins had had nothing to do with revealing her secret. But she telephoned each one nevertheless to find out. Both stoutly denied having told anyone the girls' plans except their parents. Mr. and Mrs. Marvin and Mr. and Mrs. Fayne also declared they had not mentioned the trip to any outsider.

Frowning, Nancy returned to Ned and read for herself the article in the newspaper. "Oh, my goodness!" she exclaimed suddenly. "It even says the heirloom has been reported lost or misplaced by Lady Douglas."

"I'll bet," said Ned, "that the story came from Scotland to somebody over here. And that somebody is the enemy who has been bothering you."

Ned looked at Nancy intently for several seconds. Then he said, "Nancy, do you want to go to Scotland very much?"

"Of course I do. Why do you ask?"

To her astonishment, the young man revealed that just before leaving his home in Mapleton to come to River Heights, he had received an anonymous telephone call.

"A man, evidently disguising his voice, said to me, 'If you expect to keep your girl friend alive, don't let her go to Scotland!' "

It was Nancy's turn to stare. She realized the gravity and danger of the situation, and though she assured Ned the threat would not keep her home, she admitted it made her very uneasy.

"I'm going to phone the *Graphic* office," Nancy declared. "They must know who's responsible for this story, and the source of it."

The answer was quite unsatisfactory. The young woman who took Nancy's call said that practically everybody in the news office had gone home and she was not at liberty to give out any information. In a bored tone she added, "Phone in the morning." Then she hung up.

During dinner the newspaper article and the sinister warning to Ned were discussed at length.

"Did you notice the article *didn't* say a theft is suspected?" Nancy remarked.

"That's right," Mr. Drew agreed. "It seems strange that it didn't mention such an idea."

His daughter suggested that it was possible the person who had given out the story knew the heirloom had been stolen. If everyone was led to believe the jewelry had been lost or misplaced, then neither the police nor anyone else would think of looking for a thief.

"Good reasoning," said Mr. Drew.

Nancy turned to Ned. "Since we're leaving early in the morning, I won't be able to find out anything from the *Graphic* before we go. How about your taking on that job?"

Ned laughed. "Wouldn't you be surprised if I solved the mystery on this side of the ocean?"

Nancy giggled. "I dare you! But anyway, I'm sure you *will* play a big part in doing just that!"

"Thanks for your confidence, Detective Drew," Ned replied. "Any further assignments?"

"Perhaps. There is something you should know." She told about the bomb and the shattered note in the mailbox.

As Ned whistled in astonishment, Nancy went on, "I made a tracing of the note. Before you go

I'll give it to you. Maybe you can find the person who wrote it."

Nancy also told Ned about Johnny Barto. "If you have a chance, you might drive over to see him."

"I'll do that."

Later, as he was about to say good night to Nancy, Ned told her he was spending the night with an aunt in town and would drive the Drews, Bess, and George to the airport. "Wonderful! We'll be ready on the dot of seven."

Next morning Ned arrived promptly, and helped stow the Drews' baggage. Nancy gave Hannah Gruen an affectionate hug and kiss, then they were off.

Bess and George were waiting on the sidewalk outside the Marvin home with their bags. When the three girls were settled in the rear seat, they looked at one another and burst into laughter.

Bess said, "We're three bluebirds!" The cousins and Nancy wore navy-blue coats and shoes.

Under Nancy's coat was a dark-blue-and-green striped sports dress which set off the shade of her hair to perfection. Blond Bess wore a two-piece powder-blue suit, while George had on a navy skirt and tailored white blouse.

At the airport Ned exchanged good-bys with the girls and Mr. Drew. To Nancy the youth whispered, "Don't forget—be back by June tenth!"

She gave him a quick kiss. "I'll do my best!"

Not long afterward, the plane took off for New York. During the trip Nancy brought her chums up to date on the mystery.

"It sounds dangerous to me!" said Bess. "I'll concentrate on the beautiful scenery of Scotland."

George retorted, "And while you're daydreaming, one of the villains may sneak up from behind and kidnap you, fair cousin!" Bess looked worried, but Nancy grinned.

Upon their arrival in New York, Mr. Drew announced that he had business to attend to and would have to meet the girls just before the evening plane took off for Scotland.

"You're going up to see your Aunt Eloise, aren't you, Nancy?" he asked.

"Yes, I am. Bess and George are going along."

Miss Eloise Drew, a schoolteacher, was Mr. Drew's sister. She was exceedingly fond of Nancy and her friends, and often entertained them. Nancy had phoned her aunt, who was having a half-holiday. When the three girls arrived at her uptown apartment, the tall, attractive woman, who looked very much like Nancy, welcomed the trio warmly.

"It's wonderful to see you! I do wish you could stay longer," she said.

Nancy grinned. "Since we can't, we'll just have to talk fast and cover a lot of ground!"

News was exchanged and Miss Drew was horrified to hear of possible dangers awaiting Nancy in Scotland. "Promise me you won't take any chances," she begged.

As Nancy did so, Miss Drew got up, opened a table drawer, and took out a long, narrow ebony object. Chuckling, she said, "This is a chanter from a bagpipe. Recently I attended a performance of bagpipe players and dancers, so I decided it would be fun trying to play a tune on one of these."

"How thrilling!" cried Bess. "Please play it."

Miss Drew laughed. She took out an instruction book, put the instrument to her lips, and played a tuneful phrase. "That's the first part of *Scots, Wha Hae*," she explained.

"Why, Aunt Eloise, you're marvelous!" said Nancy. "By the way, what does *Scots, Wha Hae* mean?"

With a twinkle in her eye, Aunt Eloise recited the first two lines of the song, using the broad Scottish accent of the lowlands:

> " *'Scots, wha hae wi' Wallace bled,*
> *Scots, wham Bruce has aften led.'* "

Miss Drew told them that the song was composed by Robert Burns, the Scottish poet, to commemorate the Battle of Bannockburn fought in 1314. "Unfortunately," she added, "the battles were very bloody. The words mean:

> " *'Scots, who have bled with Wallace,*
> *Scots, whom Bruce has often led.'* "

"May I try the chanter?" Nancy requested.

"Yes, indeed, but first I'll show you what the notes are and how you hold your fingers."

Nancy adjusted her hands properly, then Aunt Eloise said, "Now just blow into the chanter, raising your various fingers. Don't try any tunes until you get used to moving your fingers."

At first Nancy could not hold the chanter and play it at the same time, so her aunt suggested that she sit down and let the lower end of the instrument rest in her lap. In a few moments Nancy was playing the scales quite creditably. She asked Bess and George if they would like to take a turn, but both declined.

"I dare you to try *Scots, Wha Hae,*" George teased.

"Play it first without the grace notes," Miss Drew advised. "Of course, they're what give the charm to the music of bagpipes."

In a few minutes Nancy was playing the melody of *Scots, Wha Hae,* and after some more practice she was able, by following the instruction book, to add the grace notes to the first phrase.

"Why, it really sounds like something!" said Bess. "I never thought you'd do it!"

Nancy was quite pleased herself. "I'll try it again later." She grinned.

Just before the girls said good-by to Aunt Eloise, Nancy picked up the chanter and played the first phrase of *Scots, Wha Hae* several times.

Her aunt laughed. "It's a nice way to spend time," she said. "Perhaps while you're in Scotland you can learn more tunes."

"I doubt it," said George. "If Nancy's to find her missing heirloom and the men who are stealing sheep, she'll be kept much too busy!"

"I wish you every success," said Aunt Eloise. "But again, girls, please be careful."

Nancy and her friends hurried back to International Airport. Mr. Drew was waiting and they immediately boarded the plane. It was a luxuriously furnished one, with comfortable seats. Dinner was served, and shortly afterward the girls settled back to go to sleep. Their arrival in Scotland was scheduled for six A.M. by Greenwich time equivalent to one A.M. in the eastern part of the United States.

As passengers awakened, George found it very difficult to arouse Bess. She was completely confused as to where she was, and insisted that it was not yet time to get up.

Finally, however, when she saw rolls and hot drinks being served, Bess became her cheerful self. Often teased about her weight, she frequently declared, "I'm going to begin dieting—tomorrow."

The girls were just starting breakfast when suddenly the plane began to toss violently. The girls felt a chill of fear. Had something gone wrong with the jetliner?

CHAPTER V

An Angry Guest

THE plane continued its tossing. Bess, speechless with fear, closed her eyes, while Nancy and George gripped their chair arms.

As cups and dishes flew in every direction, their contents spattered passengers and seats. Then the jetliner suddenly leveled off.

The captain explained apologetically, "Our automatic pilot is malfunctioning. We will continue our journey on manual control."

The girls heaved sighs of relief. There were no more scares and soon the plane was circling in for a landing at Prestwick International Airport.

"We're in Scotland!" George exulted. "Now our sleuthing begins!"

Bess frowned. "Oh, George! Can't we enjoy this lovely country without being reminded of villains?"

The others laughed as they walked into the

terminal to claim their bags and have their passports checked. When they left the building, Mr.
Drew hailed a taxi. Its driver, a man of about
forty, had black hair, high color, and a pleasant
smile. He said his name was Donald Clark. Mr.
Drew asked him to drive them to Glasgow, and
climbed in front.

The three girls, seated in the rear, were delighted with Donald's broad accent and keen sense
of humor. As he pointed out various sights, he
would sometimes quote from Robert Burns's
poems.

"Ye must get up to Bobby's cottage," he said.
"And up there ye'll be seein' the Brig o' Doon."

"Oh, that's the famous bridge Tam o' Shanter
rode over, isn't it?" Nancy asked.

"That it be." Donald chuckled. "A man can
think of funny things when he lets his imagination
get the better of him. Poor Tam—he near killed
his naig makin' him go sae fast to get awa' frae
the witch hangin' on to his tail."

As the taxi reached the outskirts of Glasgow,
Nancy and the cousins were intrigued by the
numerous flocks of sea gulls. Donald told them
that the birds followed the ocean-going ships to
eat refuse thrown overboard. The girls were
also interested in the rows of old stone houses
with their many clay chimney pots. On one house
they counted nine!

When Nancy mentioned this to Donald, he told

her that the houses had no central heating. Each room had its own fireplace.

"And the apartment houses—you can look right through the center hall to the rear garden," Nancy remarked.

The taxi driver grinned. "Most of my American passengers have never heard of our open closes and closed closes," he said.

When Mr. Drew and the girls looked utterly blank, Donald added, "Our tenements—ye call them apartment houses—have a common entrance, called a close. If it has a door, it's a closed close. If it has no door, it's an open close."

Nancy remarked with a smile, "I see we have a great deal to learn in your country. We shall probably find ourselves making mistakes and people misunderstanding us."

"Aye, and that ye will!" Donald assured them.

He drove his passengers to an attractive hotel next to the railroad station and they alighted. Nancy, Bess, and George waited patiently in the lobby while Mr. Drew went up to the reservations desk to announce their arrival. After nearly ten minutes had gone by, Nancy wondered what was causing the delay. To her surprise, her father seemed to be arguing with the clerk. She overheard the lawyer say, "But you have my cable!"

Finally the clerk shrugged, produced two keys, and summoned a porter. On the way up in the elevator, Mr. Drew explained to the girls that apparently the hotel had marked his reservation Dewar, pronounced Dew-ar, instead of Drew. The lawyer's room was some distance up the hall from the one the girls would be occupying.

"After we unpack, I'll get in touch with you about my day's plans," he said as they stepped from the elevator.

Nancy, Bess, and George were delighted with their room. It was large and tastefully furnished. There was an adjoining bath, and Bess declared she had never seen such big Turkish towels in her life. "They must be seven feet long!" she exclaimed.

Nancy, meanwhile, had gone to the bureau and opened the top drawer to put away some clothes. Staring up at her was a very strange note.

"George! Bess! Come here!" she called. "The mystery has followed us!"

The cousins dashed to Nancy's side and stared at the paper. "What kind of message is that?" asked George, and read aloud the strange words:

" 'RATHAD DIG GLAS SLAT LONG

MALL BEAN BALL GUN AIL.' "

"And what weird drawings!" Bess remarked.

In the upper left-hand corner of the paper was a bagpipe. Opposite this was a cradle in the form of a boat. And at the lower left, crowding the margin, was what looked to be a part of a one-story modern building.

Bess burst into laughter. "Mystery nothing! Some kid who stayed in this room made it."

George nodded. "The words sure sound like baby talk."

Nancy was inclined to disagree, but before she could comment, the room telephone rang. She answered it, expecting the caller to be her father. To her surprise, the desk clerk was on the wire. His voice sounded excited.

"Is this Miss Drew?"

"Yes."

"I'm most frightfully sorry," he said, "but I have given you and your friends the wrong room. I will send up a porter at once for your bags. He will take you to your new room."

When Nancy reported this to the others, Bess sighed. "I'm glad I didn't start unpacking. But I'm surprised that a hotel as fine as this one would make such a mistake."

Nancy went back to concentrate on the note. Her photographic mind made a mental picture of it and she memorized the strange words.

As the young sleuth closed the bureau drawer she said, "This note may have been intended for the person who is coming into this room."

"You mean it's in code?" George asked.

"It could be," Nancy answered.

By this time the porter had arrived with a baggage truck. The girls' new quarters were still farther down the hall in the opposite direction from Mr. Drew's room. After the trio was settled, Nancy remarked, "I'll have to tell my father we've moved." To the porter, she said, "Did Mr. Dewar show up to claim that room we left?"

"Yes, ma'am, he did, and he was black wi' rage when he learned ye'd been in his room!"

Bess laughed. "I suppose he thought we'd dropped face powder all over the place!"

Nancy doubted that this was the cause of his annoyance. She could not get the strange note out of her mind. Had Mr. Dewar's anger been caused by fear that the girls had seen it? The note might be a secret message meant only for him! Later she discussed this theory with her father at the luncheon table.

"That's possible," the lawyer agreed. "But even in perfectly legitimate business deals, codes are often used, so this may not indicate that anything is wrong."

Nancy was not convinced. "The note that was left in our mailbox in River Heights said 'Drew is going to bomb you.' Do you suppose that the person who tried to warn us got Dewar and Drew mixed up?"

"My goodness, Nancy!" said George. "Your theories certainly are way out today!"

Bess leaned forward. "There's one person who is mighty interested in what you're saying. That man at the table near us—the one who's alone.

He has been trying hard to hear every word."

Nancy turned to get a look at the stranger. He was about forty years of age, well built, and had a noticeably reddish complexion. Now he quickly averted his gaze, hastily signed his check, and left the table.

Nancy's group had practically finished eating and she asked to be excused. Before the waitress could pick up the check on the stranger's table, Nancy sidled past and took a look at the check. The man had scribbled on it the number of the room which the girls had just vacated!

"He must be Mr. Dewar," Nancy thought. The others met her in the lobby and she told them of her discovery. The stranger was not around.

"You may be on a completely wrong trail, Nancy," Mr. Drew said. "I advise you not to jump to conclusions about this man. I'm going to start on my business conferences this afternoon. Why don't you girls rent a car and do some sight-seeing?"

"All right," Nancy agreed. "Where do you suggest that we go?"

"How about asking the head porter? He'll know the interesting spots and can give you the name of a rental agency. Perhaps he'll even engage a car for you and have it brought to the door."

After her father had left, Nancy approached the porter's desk. She made her request and the man said he would be very glad to make the arrangements. He asked Nancy to wait while he telephoned about hiring a small car.

"Do you have an international driver's license?" the porter asked.

"Yes."

He telephoned to an agency which promised to deliver a small car to the hotel within half an hour.

"Have you ever been to Loch Lomond?" the porter asked the girls. Learning that they had not, he said he would recommend visiting the loch as a highlight of their tour. "On the way," the man added, "I suggest a stop at the University of Glasgow, which is old and famous. And take your raincoats. Scotland's weather is apt to change quickly."

The porter brought out a map and penciled directions before handing it to Nancy.

"I hope you have a good time," he said. "And don't forget the left-side-of-the-road driving."

Nancy assured him she would be very careful. Half an hour later the three girls were in the car and setting off for the university. The campus was extensive and the gray stone buildings impressive. They were very symmetrical, with a fine balance of towers.

Nancy finally drove out of the city and found the road to Loch Lomond. When they reached the country area, Bess exclaimed, "What a lovely landscape! Don't you adore those bushy hedges? Nancy, stop! I want to see what they are."

Nancy pulled to the side of the road. "They're rose brier and hawthorn," she said. "They must be beautiful when they're in bloom."

She drove on and presently George noticed some monkey puzzle trees and remarked on their twisted, interwoven limbs. "How sparse their foliage is, compared to the oaks and elms!"

"Speaking of monkeys, Nancy, we haven't had any real bad luck on this trip," Bess said. "Maybe we should thank that monkey pin Ned gave you."

All three girls laughed, but suddenly worried looks came over their faces.

"Look out, Nancy!" George warned. "That car coming toward us is on the wrong side of the road! The driver must be an American!"

Nancy honked her horn wildly, but the driver paid no attention. Nancy was trying to decide what to do. If she stayed where she was, there would certainly be an accident. But if she moved to the opposite side of the road, the other driver might suddenly do the same thing!

Bess was terrified. She shrieked, "That man's going to crash into us!"

CHAPTER VI

Houseboat Victims

THE oncoming driver seemed to have no intention of moving to the other side of the road.

"I'll have to pull off!" Nancy concluded quickly. In a split second she deliberately plowed into a hedge and stopped. At almost the same moment the stranger yanked his steering wheel, swerving his small, closed car into his left lane.

As he whizzed past the girls, the man held his right hand up in such a way that it shielded his face.

"He's crazy!" George said angrily.

"Not so crazy that he'd let us see who he is," Bess stormed.

Nancy sat still without saying a word. She had not yet recovered from her fright. Ruefully she looked out the window at the ruined section of hedge.

"I suppose I'll have to pay for the damage,"

Nancy thought, and turned to look back at the house they had just passed. It was a small, quaint stone structure with an arched entranceway.

Bess and George were still talking about the near accident. George had tried to get the license number of the other car, but had caught only part of it: GB-2.

By this time Nancy had recovered her equilibrium, and now speculated on the identity of the driver who had tried to ram them.

Suddenly Bess spoke up. "Nancy! Remember that threatening note with the Scotch plaid? Do you think this could be another attempt to damage a car of yours?"

"It could very well be," Nancy agreed. "Even if that driver was on the wrong side of the road by mistake, my horn should have warned him."

At that moment the door of the stone house opened and a woman of about fifty bustled up to the girls. She was rather plump, had high color in her cheeks, and her black hair was pulled straight back with a knot at the nape of her neck. Her expression was severe but not unfriendly.

Immediately Nancy and her friends stepped from the car. Nancy introduced the three, and the woman said she was Mrs. Gilmer.

"I'm dreadfully sorry this happened," Nancy told her apologetically. "Actually it was not my fault. I had to avoid a bad accident." She told about the oncoming driver and how he had swerved at the last moment. Tire marks in the road attested her statement. "I will be very glad to pay for the damage, however."

The woman's expression changed to one of kindness. "Nae, nae, I'm just glad ye're all safe." She went into a tirade about drivers that raced up and down this stretch of road "as if Tam o' Shanter's witch was after them." The girls smiled.

"I'll back the car out," Nancy offered. "Then we can see how much of the hedge is broken."

The damage proved not to be extensive and Mrs. Gilmer said, "I canna charge ye a farthing. Ye are Americans and obeying our laws. Ye shouldna' suffer for the daft actions of someone else."

Bess was on the verge of blurting out their suspicions about the driver, but thought better of it and kept still. Nancy thanked Mrs. Gilmer. Smiling, she added, "Left-side-of-the-road driving has always puzzled me. How did the custom start?"

The Scotswoman said the only explanation she had ever heard was that in ancient times the roads were not very safe for horsemen because of brigands.

" 'Tis said a rider would hold the reins in the left hand, and keep a sword in the right ready to deal with any highwayman coming on horseback from the opposite direction."

"Ugh!" said Bess. "I'm glad I didn't live in those dangerous times!"

Mrs. Gilmer smiled. "I guess it actually wasna' any more dangerous than it is now, as ye all found out!"

The girls said good-by to her and set off once more for Loch Lomond. The drive was most pleasant, leading past several big estates with high stone walls screening them from the road.

Presently George called out, "I see the lake!"

"Loch," Bess corrected her.

"Isn't it lovely!" Nancy exclaimed.

Bess sighed. "Loch Lomond is just as beautiful as the songs and stories about it."

As far as the girls could see, the crystal-clear water was surrounded by wooded hills. Islands dotted the surface of the loch.

Nancy had pulled up beside a cove and sat staring ahead at a row of houseboats. They looked like huge square boxes with windows. All were one story high and painted white. Each was secured to its own dock.

"Girls," Nancy said excitedly, "those houseboats remind me of one of the pictures on that strange note we found in the hotel room!"

"Me too!" George agreed. "But do you think a houseboat has anything to do with our mystery?"

Nancy shrugged. "I'm going to keep it in mind as a clue."

Bess, meanwhile, had been looking at the sky. What had started out to be a bright day was now an overcast one, with dark clouds scudding over the sun. The wind had picked up considerably.

"Maybe we'd better not go much farther," she suggested. "If a storm breaks, I'd just as soon get back to the hotel. Wouldn't you?"

Nancy agreed and said she would drive only a short distance. In the main, the road kept fairly close to the water. At one point near the shore a small stone pedestal had been erected. At the top was the statue of a small boy.

"I wonder why it was put there," said George.

"I read about it in a guidebook," Nancy answered. "The poor little fellow was drowned at this spot, so his parents erected the statue in his memory."

"How sad!" Bess murmured.

The wind began to blow in great gusts and when the girls reached the small town of Luss, Nancy decided to turn around. At times the car shivered in the blasts. Nancy almost had to fight the wheel to keep in her lane.

"Let's hurry!" Bess urged. "I don't like this!"

Nancy put on more speed. By the time they reached the cove where the houseboats were tied up, the wind was blowing with gale force. The large craft were rocking violently.

"I sure wouldn't want to be living in one of those," George remarked. "Not in this weather."

*Could they get close enough to the houseboat to
assist the trapped victims?*

Suddenly a tremendous rush of wind came directly at them from the loch. It actually forced the car to the other side of the road! Nancy jammed on her brakes and the car held its position.

Bess and George, meanwhile, were watching the tossing houseboats. Suddenly Bess gave a shriek.

"One of the boats is going over!"

Nancy turned to look. The gale had lifted the third houseboat out of the water and sent it crashing onto the beach! The next second it toppled over! The girls could hear screams and cries above the howling wind.

"There are people in it! We must do something to help them!" Nancy exclaimed.

Without thinking of the danger to themselves, the three girls took their raincoats and hats from the rear seat and quickly pulled them on. Nancy had shut off the engine and put on the hand brake.

Opening the door was like pushing against a gigantic wave, but the girls finally managed it and struggled out sideways. By this time rain was falling in a sheet. Loch Lomond was being whipped into white foam and small boats in the cove were tossing wildly.

As the girls endeavored to go forward along the shore, the screams from within the overturned houseboat increased. Could they get close enough to assist the trapped victims? No one had appeared from the other craft. Were their occupants away or afraid to come outside?

As the girls plowed toward the overturned boat, Bess gave a shout of alarm. She was behind the others, who turned quickly.

Nancy and George were horrified to see the force of the wind pushing Bess rapidly toward the angry water! Unable to keep her balance, she fell in headlong, the churning water crashing over her!

CHAPTER VII

The Dungeon

IN a flash, Nancy and George splashed into the whipping water of Loch Lomond and went to Bess's assistance. She tried twice to get up, only to be knocked over again by a lashing wave.

Reaching her side, the two rescuers helped her stand up, though their own footing was precarious. Arm in arm, the three struggled to the beach.

Bess sank down. "Th-thanks for saving me."

"Do you want to go back to the car?" Nancy asked her. "George and I can investigate the houseboat."

"No, no," Bess replied quickly. "I'm all right. I want to help the poor people in there."

Above the wind the girls could hear a child crying, "Mama! Mama! Wake up!"

The three hurried forward and clambered onto the side of the overturned houseboat. There was no door but Nancy managed to open a window, and leaned down over the sill. She surveyed what was below her. Furniture and rugs lay scattered on the opposite wall, which now formed the floor of the houseboat. Stretched out was a woman and beside her knelt a little girl, sobbing.

The child looked up at Nancy. "Did you come to wake my mama up?" she asked.

Nancy gazed at the tear-stained face. She fervently hoped that the little girl's mother was only unconscious.

"I'm coming, honey," Nancy replied. Calling to her friends, she quickly described the scene below, then said, "Give me a hand so I can drop gently."

The cousins crawled over. Each held one of Nancy's hands as she eased her body downward.

"Okay. Let go!" she said.

Nancy hastened to the woman. After a quick examination she reported that the little girl's mother apparently had not suffered any broken bones. Probably she had struck her head when the boat tipped over.

"I'll put this table under the window," Nancy said to Bess and George. "Then you won't have so far to jump." She righted the sturdy pine table and helped steady George when she dropped. Then both girls assisted Bess down.

The child was crying and trying to hide behind an upended overstuffed chair. Bess went to her at once. "What's your name?"

"Isa Arden. Pl-please make my mama wake up!"

"We will," Bess promised. "Do come out and see me."

The little girl's shyness vanished. She ran to Bess. "Everything's upside down!" she wailed.

"It will be all right soon," Bess assured her.

Meanwhile, Nancy and George had been trying to revive Mrs. Arden. Nancy chafed the woman's wrists and massaged the back of her neck, while George hunted for a stimulant. Finally she found a bottle of camphor, which she waved under Mrs. Arden's nose until the woman regained consciousness.

She rubbed her head, then in a weak voice asked, "Who are you? Where am I?"

"Mama! Mama!" Isa cried joyfully, and rushed over to hug her mother.

In a few seconds the whole catastrophe came back to Mrs. Arden. "You came to help us?" she asked the girls. "You saw the accident?"

"Yes," said Nancy. She introduced herself and Bess and George. "The wind and rain have died down. Can we take you to some neighbor?"

At that moment a man poked his head through the window and called down, "Mrs. Arden, be ye all right?"

"Aye. These kind lassies have offered to help Isa and me get out."

The man put his arms through the opening

and said, "Hand Isa up. My wife is with me. She'll take care of her."

As soon as the child had been lifted out, the girls boosted Mrs. Arden to the opening, where the man helped her climb through it.

The three girls then scrambled outside. The neighbors introduced themselves as Mr. and Mrs. Scott. When they saw the bedraggled condition of the Americans, they invited them to come into their houseboat and dry off.

"We'd be glad to accept," Nancy said quickly.

The Scotts' houseboat was neat and cozy, with everything in its proper place. The girls' clothing soon dried from the warmth of a stove. After the three had washed their faces and hands and combed their hair, Mrs. Scott suddenly looked intently at Nancy.

"Why, your picture is on the cover of *Photographie Internationale!*" she exclaimed. "I thought your name seemed familiar when you introduced yourself. You're the American girl detective!"

Nancy blushed, not because of the praise, but because she knew the news of her presence had been broadcast in Scotland. "I'll probably be recognized almost everywhere!" she groaned inwardly. "Whoever my enemy is, he will be alerted as to where I am and keep out of my way! How can I ever catch him!"

"If you're looking for mysteries, we have one

right here," Mrs. Scott went on. "Did you notice that the last houseboat is some distance away from the others?"

"No, I didn't," Nancy admitted.

Mrs. Scott lowered her voice. "Some very strange-acting men live on it now. The couple who stay there summers don't arrive until later. They must have rented their houseboat to these men. But nobody around here has even found out what their names are. They mostly come and go at night, and don't seem to have a car."

Nancy was intrigued. She said, "Unless we can do something else for Mrs. Arden and Isa, I think we'd better leave. First, though, I'll walk up and take a look at that houseboat."

Nancy would have liked to ask more questions, but a group of neighbors arrived and there was no chance. The three girls exchanged farewells with the Scotts and Ardens, then made their way to the last houseboat. They stepped from the dock onto a narrow deck which circled the craft. The windows were heavily curtained and there was no answer to their knock. The trio walked around the deck, but found no clues to cast suspicion on the occupants.

"Let's go!" Bess pleaded. "I can't wait to have a hot bath and put on clean clothes."

"Bess," Nancy said sympathetically, "you must have been horribly uncomfortable all this time. I'll get you to Glasgow in a jiffy!"

When they arrived at the hotel, Nancy changed into a fresh dress, then decided to tell her father of their afternoon's experience and her suspicions. Bess and George declared they would rest for a while. As Nancy passed the room to which she and her friends had first been assigned, she heard a bagpipe being played. The tune was *Scots, Wha Hae!*

She paused to listen. The piper was apparently a beginner, for he was going over and over the first phrase and not playing it very well.

"I wonder if that's Mr. Dewar!" Nancy walked on, recalling the message in the bureau drawer. One of the sketches on it was that of a bagpipe! Was there a connection between the two circumstances?

Nancy knocked on the door of her father's room and was delighted to find him there. Mr. Drew was reading an evening paper. "Here's something you're not going to like, I'm afraid," he told his daughter. On the front page was a picture of Nancy taken from the cover of *Photographie Internationale,* and a story which called her "the girl detective tourist." Seeing it, she groaned. "This is horrible, Dad! I don't want to be recognized!"

She told him of the houseboat episode and how Mrs. Scott had identified her. "Soon I won't be able to do any sleuthing in secret."

Her father expressed his concern, and then, to

lighten Nancy's spirits, he said with a grin, "It's almost like wearing a uniform and a badge. I think I'll get you one marked 'Detective'!"

Nancy laughed but in a moment became sober again as she told of the near accident on the road. Mr. Drew frowned. "It certainly looks as if the fellow deliberately tried to give you a bad scare—if not to injure you. I wish we could find out who is behind these car episodes."

"I'm sure the missing heirloom has something to do with it," she replied. "Dad, do you think we should notify the police?"

After a few moments' thought, the lawyer decided against it. "We really have nothing to go on," he said. "You didn't get the full license number of the car, and you can't identify the driver. I do have one suggestion. Let's not eat in the hotel dining room. There's a French restaurant next door. Suppose we go there about seven and find a secluded table."

"That sounds great, Dad," said Nancy.

Mr. Drew and the girls found the restaurant to be delightful. At the lawyer's request the attentive headwaiter seated them in an alcove. No one bothered them, but Nancy did notice that their waiter, and also the bus boy, stared intently at her several times.

She began to suspect that they had recognized her. As they were eating dessert, the bus boy handed her a piece of paper and a pencil.

"Monsieur, at the second table from here, would like the autograph of the girl detective."

It took Nancy only a split second to decide not to accede to the request. She was remembering the man called Pete in River Heights who had paid a dollar for her signature. She was not going to give anybody else a chance to use her autograph in some unsavory scheme.

Nancy looked over at "Monsieur." She smiled graciously, shook her head, and with her lips formed the word "Sorry."

Mr. Drew paid the check and the foursome left hurriedly. They went back to the hotel and up to their rooms. At the girls' door Nancy's father said, "Be ready to leave for Edinburgh early in the morning. I've engaged the driver we had yesterday—Donald Clark. The hotel will prepare a lunch for us to take along."

Before leaving next morning, Nancy went to the desk and asked if Mr. Dewar were still registered.

"No, he checked out very early this morning."

As Nancy joined the others in the taxi she thought, "I have a strong hunch Mr. Dewar's path and mine will cross again."

Donald was his same cheery self, and asked if his passengers had any errands in town before they set off for Edinburgh.

Nancy spoke up. "If we have time, I'd like to go to a bagpipe factory and see how the instruments are made." She chuckled. "Perhaps if I find out, I can learn to play better!"

Mr. Drew said there was plenty of time, so Donald took them into the heart of Glasgow's business district, where the factory was located. It manufactured not only bagpipes but the proper costumes for men to wear while marching and playing. The visitors were astounded to learn that every tartan used by any Scottish clan could be purchased here.

"Girls rarely play bagpipes," said the factory guide who was taking them around. "Instead, they get all decked out in their blouses and plaid skirts to do our native dances."

"Where could I purchase a girl's outfit?" Nancy asked. The man gave her the name of a shop in the city. Nancy turned to her father. "I'd love to have a Douglas tartan," she said.

Mr. Drew grinned. "We'll get you a costume right after we leave here."

The guide led the visitors from room to room. He showed them the sheepskin bag which the piper filled with air to be used as needed while he was playing. The bag was covered with cloth made of the player's tartan.

Next, the group was shown the various wooden parts of the bagpipes. The chanter, which produced the tune, had a reed at the top. At the lower end was a rubber valve, which closed when necessary to prevent air escaping from the bag.

Besides the chanter there were three pipes for accompaniment. They were called drones. Two of these were tenor and one bass.

The guide explained, "All the pipes are made of hard African blackwood. The ivory that trims the pipes comes from India, and the canes for the reeds that go into the pipes are from Spain. All the parts are screwed together."

The splitting of the pale-yellow reeds proved to be the most interesting part of the tour for Nancy. She learned that the cane was very carefully split partway down to give just the proper sound.

A little later Nancy's group thanked the guide for his informative talk. As they left the factory, Bess remarked, "It's all too complicated for me. I'll stick to the piano!"

Donald drove to the shop where Nancy was to purchase her Douglas tartan outfit. She tried it on and was pleased. "I'd like to wear it, but I'd certainly attract attention," Nancy said to the girls. She had not seen a single Scottish girl wearing tartans. Nancy mentioned this to Donald when she returned to the car.

"Up in the Highlands," he said, "ye will see the lassies in them. Don't ye be afraid to wear yours there."

As they rode along, he suggested that they visit Stirling Castle. " 'Tis a bit out o' the way, but I think ye'll feel well rewarded."

The girls and Mr. Drew said they would like to go. When they approached the castle, George exclaimed, "What a fabulous place!" A cluster of impressive stone buildings stood on a high hill.

Two guards in colorful kilts were stationed at either side of the entrance. Just inside, a guide was waiting to escort the party. He led the way up a steep cobblestone driveway to a plaza around which were grouped the various buildings.

"That smallest one used to be a mint," the guide pointed out. "Silver from nearby hills was made into coin of the realm. Some people say that was the origin of sterling silver!"

The visitors were fascinated by the elaborately furnished kings' rooms, and the smaller apartment used by the famous Mary, Queen of Scots, before her imprisonment in England. But the guide told so many stories of loyal subjects, mixed with the gory details of intrigues and double-crossing deals of history, that the girls' heads were swimming.

Names which caught Nancy's attention, however, were those of the great heroes of the country—William Wallace and Robert Bruce. *"Scots, Wha Hae* was composed in their honor!" she recalled.

As the visitors went outside, Bess sighed. "Poor Mary, Queen of Scots! In prison for about twenty years! And then executed!"

The guide led the group across the courtyard

to a stone stairway leading downward. "Would you like to see the dungeon below?" he asked.

"We may as well," Mr. Drew replied.

"You won't need me," said the guide. "I'll wait here."

The four tourists descended, and immediately felt the damp chill of the underground prison. When they reached the far end, Bess shivered. "This is a horrible place! I can't bear to think of the poor people who were thrown in here, when they hadn't done anything wrong except to disagree with their ruler. Let's go!"

She turned and almost ran back outside. George and Mr. Drew followed. The guide chuckled. "A wee spooky, isn't it?" Then he asked, "Where is the young lady detective? She *is* the one on the magazine cover?"

The others suddenly realized that Nancy was not with them. "I'll go get her," Mr. Drew offered. "She has probably found something unusual."

He returned in a few minutes, a worried expression on his face. "Nancy isn't down there!"

"What!" the guide exclaimed. "She must be! She hasn't come out!"

In panic, Mr. Drew, Bess, and George hastened down the steps to make a search for the missing girl. What had happened to Nancy?

CHAPTER VIII

A Confession

By this time the guide, too, had become worried. As Bess, George, and Mr. Drew reached the foot of the dungeon steps, he called down, "Wait! I'll come along. I must tell you something. Another sightseer went into the dungeon right after you did. He was mumbling something that sounded like 'I'll get her!' Maybe—maybe he meant Miss Drew, and has put her in the suffocation chamber!"

"What!" the three exclaimed in horror.

The guide explained there was a small recess in the wall of the first chamber they had entered, where prisoners of old had been suffocated in seven minutes by a huge stone being placed across the opening. The stone was still there on the floor.

He and the visitors raced pell-mell into the dungeon and went straight to the suffocation recess. The great stone lay on the ground. Nancy was not inside!

Mr. Drew heaved a sigh of relief. "Thank goodness!" he said. "Somehow Nancy must have gone out without any of us noticing."

As the group hurried back up the steps, the guide admitted he had been gone for a few minutes from the place at which he had posted himself to await their return. To their intense relief, they saw Nancy approaching them from the main entrance of the castle. The guide went off.

"Nancy, you scared us silly!" cried Bess. "Where have you been?"

The young sleuth quickly explained. "When you all were at the far end of the dungeon, I went back partway to look at something. Just then I saw a man come down the steps and walk toward me. He was that autograph snatcher in River Heights—the man named Pete!"

"Are you sure?" George asked unbelievingly.

"I'm positive!" Nancy answered. "As soon as he saw me, he turned and ran like mad. I tore after him but couldn't catch him. Right outside the entrance gate he jumped into a car that looked like the one that nearly hit us on the way to Loch Lomond. It sped off, but I'm sure the driver was the person we know as Mr. Dewar."

"So those two are in league!" said George. "That proves they're up to no good, and somehow you Drews are involved."

All this time, Bess had been staring wide-eyed at Nancy. Finally she told of the mumbling the guide had heard, and added gloomily, "I'll bet that man Pete would've pushed you into that seven-minute suffocation chamber when you weren't looking!"

George laughed scornfully. "Ridiculous! With all of us around! Nancy, why do you think he dared come into the dungeon and risk being seen?"

"My hunch is, George, that he was sent to eavesdrop on our conversation and any plans we may have. He was taken by surprise when he saw me looking directly at him."

Mr. Drew remarked that their enemies must be watching every move. "I guess your suspicions about Mr. Dewar are confirmed," the lawyer said to Nancy. "He must have overheard you girls talking in your hotel room, so he checked out ahead of us and followed Donald's car. From now on I guess you three had better talk in whispers!"

Mr. Drew asked Nancy if she had caught the license number of the fleeing car.

"Yes, I did," she said. "A guard at the castle entrance let me telephone the police. They checked, and told me it was a rented car and that after what had happened the men probably would abandon it very soon."

George was angry. "It seems to me that every

time we get near a solution—poof! It goes up in smoke!"

"Why didn't the guards stop Pete at the entrance gate?" Bess asked Nancy.

Nancy shrugged her shoulders. "I guess it all happened too fast."

The group walked to Donald's car and climbed in. They said nothing to him about the recent episode, and soon they were relaxing and enjoying his delightful talk. Presently he stopped in a pleasant spot by a shaded brook, called a burn.

"What a perfect picnic place!" Bess said.

Later, while they were eating, Donald asked, "Do ye know about the old town in Scotland where everybody had the same last name?"

"You're kidding!" said Bess.

"Nae, and that I am not," Donald replied. "The name was MacKenzie, but the people there all called one another by nicknames. Some of them were pretty daft. Once a fellow came down from the church steeple on ropes, so they called him 'The Flyer.' The chemist was nicknamed 'Shake the Bottle' and the barber—well, he got the name 'Soapy'!"

Everyone laughed, and George remarked facetiously, "I suppose the town carpenter was called 'Nails.'"

"We call him a joiner," said Donald. He chuckled. "If he dinna' join things right and hit his thumb, we'd call him stupid!"

The picnic ended and the debris was put back into the lunch box to be disposed of later. The sightseers resumed their journey. As they went through the town of Falkirk somewhat later, Donald turned east toward the Firth of Forth.

George said, "In our country, I suppose we would call this a bay," and Mr. Drew nodded.

When they reached Bo'ness, Donald drew up before a large brown stone plaque wedged into the hillside. On it was a long inscription in Latin.

"This was one of the Roman walls," said the Scotsman. "It originally ran for thirty miles from here to the River Clyde. The wall was twelve feet high, and a deep trench was built on the enemy's side to keep soldiers from climbing over the wall."

Nancy was endeavoring to make out the somewhat faint letters in the inscription, and managed to learn that the wall had been built during the reign of the Roman Emperor, Antoninus Pius.

"Oh, dear!" Bess gave a sigh. "It seems to me that all day long I've been learning about wars, bloodshed, and horrible punishments."

Donald looked at her understandingly. "Perhaps we should go. I promise not to tell another story about cruelty today."

Bess smiled. "Thanks!"

When they were seated in the car once more and heading toward Edinburgh, Donald asked, "Did ye ever hear about the naval commander who was ordered to anchor his ship at the Forth Bridge?"

The others shook their heads and Donald went on, "Actually, the Forth Bridge runs from outside of Edinburgh across the Firth. Well, this captain kept goin' and goin' and finally radioed back: 'Where is the *fourth* bridge? I can only find one!' "

"Good story!" said Nancy as everyone chuckled.

In a few minutes Donald said, "Schoolboys in Scotland are given a riddle. 'How many inches in the Forth?'

"They guess varying depths of water but are finally told, 'There are only seven.' Of course they all say no big ships could travel in seven inches of water. Then the person who is teasing them will say, 'But an inch, laddie, is an island!' "

"Oooh!" cried Bess. "Donald, how could you?"

Their driver grinned, then stopped talking, since traffic was becoming heavy. By the time they reached Edinburgh the evening rush hour was at its height. The streets were crowded with pedestrians and vehicles.

The American visitors admired the fine buildings and the extremely clean streets. "Isn't this a lovely city!" Nancy murmured.

Donald drove up the broad main avenue, with its attractive shops on one side and lovely park on the other. On a hill beyond stood the imposing castle. Presently the group reached the hotel where they were to stay. Like the one in Glasgow, it was next to the huge railroad station.

The four travelers were genuinely sorry to say good-by to Donald. "Thank you for a wonderful trip," said Nancy. The others expressed their appreciation also.

" 'Twas a pleasure driving ye." Donald grinned. "I wish ye all luck and happiness."

With that, he waved and drove off. Mr. Drew and the girls entered the hotel. In a lounge off the lobby, tea was being served. "Just what I need after that long ride," Bess declared, eyeing the luscious-looking pastries contained in a multiple-tiered cart. She walked into the room.

The other girls followed, while Mr. Drew registered for them all and sent the baggage to their rooms. They spent the next half hour eating the various dainty cakes and sipping the delicious tea.

When they had finished, George said, "Mr. Drew, there'll be only three of us at dinner tonight." When he inquired why, the girl's eyes twinkled and she answered, "Bess has had hers!"

"That's what you think!" her cousin retorted. "Two hours from now I'll be ready for seven courses!"

Nancy giggled. "They may serve only four!"

A little later they all went upstairs to the girls' room. As Nancy unlocked the door, the telephone was ringing. When she answered, the operator said, "Miss Drew? . . . I have an overseas call for you. One moment, please."

In a few seconds a young man's voice came over the wire and Nancy almost shrieked, "Ned!"

Bess and George grinned and nodded their heads knowingly. After an exchange of excited greetings, Ned said to Nancy, "Detective Nickerson is calling to report to Detective Drew. I have some news for you. I got hold of the *Graphic* reporter who wrote the story that went with your picture. He finally broke down and said he had learned of your plans from a man named Pete. I did some sleuthing and found out that Pete's full name is Paul Petrie!"

"Oh, marvelous!" exclaimed Nancy. "Who *is* this Mr. Petrie?"

"He lives in town. Petrie has never been in trouble with the police, but I learned that he isn't very well regarded. Had a few near brushes with the law when some of his checks bounced."

"Ned, that's clever detecting!" Nancy exclaimed.

"Wait until you hear what else I have to tell you. It's *really* big news! Nancy, I tracked down the person who wrote that warning note about the bomb!"

CHAPTER IX

Being Shadowed

As Nancy listened eagerly, Ned told her how he had located the writer of the warning note. "I studied your tracing of the writing. First, like you, I was sure a woman had written the words. You may remember Professor Webster at Emerson. Along with teaching archaeology, he's a handwriting expert. He and I have had many discussions about how the formation of letters is an indication of one's character."

"You mean," said Nancy, "a bold, vertical handwriting usually belongs to a literary person and jerky, slanted-to-the-right letters are a sign of nervousness?"

"Exactly. After studying the note you received, I figured it had been written by a somewhat shy, motherly person, probably elderly. From the type of paper used, I deduced she lived in a middle-income area of town and might shop locally. So I hounded the markets and kept my eyes open."

"And you found her that way?" Nancy asked.

Ned chuckled. "Sure did." He had taken a young cousin of his along to the various stores. "We stayed near the check-out counter," Ned went on. "Whenever an elderly woman came up to the cashier, we'd start talking about bombs and watch her reaction. Finally, in one supermarket, we saw a woman tremble violently, and asked her point-blank about the note. She admitted putting it in your mailbox."

"You're simply a genius!" Nancy exclaimed. "Go on!"

"This woman, Mrs. Morrison, runs a small rooming house. There are several within the block and many strangers come and go. But one day Mrs. Morrison was just about to close a window which opens onto an alleyway, when she heard two men talking below. One said he had had orders from Mr. Drew to use a bomb on the girl detective and her father."

"What else did she hear?" Nancy asked excitedly.

"That was about all, except the words 'He's a lawyer.' Mrs. Morrison looked out, but by this time the men had gone. She couldn't make up her mind whether they were serious or not. She was tempted to call the police, but decided against it."

"What *did* Mrs. Morrison do?"

"She casually inquired of the cashier in the supermarket if she knew of any girl detectives in town. When she heard there was one by the name of Nancy Drew, whose father was a lawyer, Mrs. Morrison became more puzzled than ever, and wondered if some family feud was being carried on between Drew and Drew.

"Finally," Ned went on, "Mrs. Morrison decided to write the warning note anonymously. She put it in your mailbox, rang the bell, and hurried away."

Nancy again praised Ned for his fine sleuthing. Then she told him about her own adventures in Scotland and of the man named Dewar.

"I'm sure now that what Mrs. Morrison overheard was the name Dewar," Nancy added.

Bess and George, meanwhile, having caught snatches of Ned's big news, could hardly wait for Nancy to finish the conversation. At last she put down the phone and told them.

"At dinner I'm going to ask Dad if we shouldn't notify the police."

"Well, I think it's about time!" said George. "The idea of that horrid Mr. Dewar trying to injure you—maybe even kill you!"

"But why would anyone want to go to such lengths?" Bess queried.

Nancy shrugged. "I figure Mr. Dewar must be the head of a gang. He's probably carrying on some kind of underhanded scheme that he doesn't want my dad and me to investigate." The young sleuth added that since one suspect, Petrie, had been in River Heights and now had met Dewar in Scotland, it was her guess that the whole affair had something to do with smuggling.

With a sigh, Bess said, "We started out with a nice little mystery. Now we're mixed up with smugglers and bomb-planters and goodness knows what else!"

Nancy and George laughed. In a few minutes Mr. Drew knocked on the girls' door and the group went downstairs to dinner. Nancy told him what she had learned from Ned. Mr. Drew agreed that the police should be notified, and Nancy did this directly after the meal. She included all aspects and possible clues in the mystery so far. The chief constable promised to try to apprehend Mr. Dewar for questioning.

The following morning the group went to church. On their return to the hotel, Nancy called headquarters once more. The superintendent on duty said, "We have no news of Mr. Dewar, but we did follow up your tip on the houseboat. I guess you were right about the occupants. By the time we got there last evening the men had left.

"Neighbors told us that earlier they had moved many large boxes and packages to a truck waiting on the road. Sounds suspicious to me. Evidently they wanted to make everything look honest, because they left money on a table with a printed note: 'This is for the rent.'"

The officer went on, "Too bad we got there so late. All the police of Scotland have been alerted. I am sure Mr. Dewar will be picked up, as well as his friend Paul Petrie."

The next day Mr. Drew had a business conference in connection with the Douglas estate, so the girls decided to visit Edinburgh Castle. They took a taxi up the steep hill leading to it.

At either side of the entrance stood a soldier. One wore a kilt, tight-buttoned jacket, and the narrow Glengarry cap with two ribbons hanging down the back. In front of the kilt hung a sporran, a slightly elongated white leather purse. The other soldier wore trousers of the regimental plaid. The men smiled at the girls as they passed through the great stone archway into the courtyard.

In the castle itself there were rooms and rooms of old armor and regimental coats. Nancy noticed an absence of kilts in the various showcases. A guard said that after the Jacobite Rebellion of 1745 when Bonnie Prince Charlie, the Young Pretender, fled from the Highlands to France, and the House of Hanover reigned over England and Scotland, the wearing of kilts was forbidden.

"This was done to keep the Highlanders from

being reminded of Scottish clans and their taste for rebellion. The custom was not revived until George III's reign."

Bess, who had overheard the conversation, remarked, "I'm glad kilts were revived. Men look so picturesque wearing them!"

After Nancy and her friends had seen most of the stately castle, they went outside to look into tiny Saint Margaret's Chapel. They learned that anyone in the armed forces of the United Kingdom, no matter what his religion, can be married there.

"Isn't that sweet!" Bess said dreamily.

As the three visitors left the courtyard, George said, "Where to next?"

Nancy, looking straight down the hilly street which led to Holyrood Palace, said, "This is called the Royal Mile. There are many famous places on the way. Let's walk down."

On the way they came to St. Giles' Cathedral and went straight to a square side room which was the Chapel of the Knights of the Thistle, the Highest Order of Chivalry.

Very tall, narrow seats, beautifully carved, were arranged side by side. Above them were the various family shields, topped by canopies and coats of arms.

Bess sighed. "Isn't it romantic? Think of all those noblemen in full regalia seated here and discussing the destiny of Scotland!"

George grinned at her cousin. "Bess, you should have lived a couple of centuries ago and been carried off by a romantic knight and had him pin a corsage of thistles on you—that's the national emblem."

Nancy smiled as the girls walked into the main part of the cathedral. The pulpit proper stood in the center with rows of benches facing it from four sides. Nancy glanced at the guidebook she was carrying.

"It says a woman was responsible for starting the 1637 civil war here. There were no pews, so each member of the congregation brought his own stool. A woman named Jenny Geddes, angry at the Bishop for the views he was proclaiming, suddenly stood up and hurled her stool at him! At once there was a commotion, and soon religious riots broke out all over Scotland."

"She was a courageous soul!" George commented.

As the trio left the fine old building, Nancy remarked, "Down the street a short way is the home of John Knox, the great reformer and preacher."

The girls hurried toward the small three-story structure and went up an outside stairway. The residence contained only display cases of letters, books, sermons written by Knox, and pictures.

"Oh, look!" Bess cried suddenly. "See how John Knox signed his name!"

Her friends stared. In a bold scrawl was written Johannes Cnoxus!

George read bits of sermons and remarked, "He was a fiery preacher, all right. I wonder if anyone today would sit still for two hours and listen to such tirades!"

She and the others went out to the street again. Bess declared she was very hungry, so they found a small restaurant above St. Giles and had luncheon. Then they continued down the Royal Mile.

About two minutes later George suddenly remarked, "I have a hunch the man back there is following us on purpose."

Nancy stole a glance at him. He had reddish hair, side whiskers, and a beard. He wore a kilt and a navy-blue balmoral.

"He looks vaguely familiar," Nancy said, "but I can't place him."

George whispered, "Let's turn and walk toward him to see what happens."

The three friends did an about-face. As the man passed them, he averted his face and went on, but in a few moments he turned and once more followed the girls.

"Suppose we cross the street and head for Holyrood again," Nancy suggested.

When the trio was on the opposite side, the red-bearded stranger soon crossed over and once more walked behind them.

"Oh, dear!" said Bess. "What'll we do?"

George grinned, and said she had a daring proposal to make. "If Nancy thinks she knows the man but doesn't recognize him, it might be because he's wearing a disguise. What say we find out if those side whiskers and beard are false!"

CHAPTER X

Gaelic Code Message

"OH, George!" Bess protested. "You wouldn't dare try pulling off that man's beard!"

"Wouldn't I!" George retorted. "If he's one of Nancy's enemies, I want to find out just who he is!"

Nancy smiled. "Thanks a million, George, but we Americans had better not cause any disturbance here. How about this idea? Why don't we separate and meet at Holyrood Palace? Mr. Redbeard can't follow all of us."

"That's a good plan," Bess agreed at once. "Since I'm sure it's you he's after, why don't you let him follow you, and George and I will follow him!"

Nancy nodded. "I'll walk on this side of the street with George. Then she can stop and pretend to look in a window and drop behind the man when he goes by. Bess, you cross over, and in case he does too, see where he goes."

The plan worked nicely until they neared the Scottish law-court buildings on Bess's side of the street. Then, suddenly, the strange man dashed into one of them.

Bess's heart was beating fast. But she took a deep gulp of air and plunged after him.

The guard at the door stopped her. "Have you a pass?" he asked.

"No, I haven't."

"Then I'm afraid I cannot let you in. The building is closed to visitors today."

Bess flushed. "I wanted to find out about the red-haired man who came in here."

The guard eyed Bess a bit suspiciously. Then he said stiffly, "I cannot tell you anything about him except that he had a pass."

Chagrined, Bess turned away. She waited for several minutes, but the bearded stranger did not reappear. She was puzzled. Why had he been following the girls if he were on legitimate business? And if he were not, how did he happen to have a pass to the building?

Disappointed that her part in the sleuthing had brought no results, Bess started down the street and finally came to the grounds of Holyrood Palace. Nancy and George were waiting.

"Any luck?" George asked her cousin.

Bess shook her head and told what had happened. "If that man isn't honest, how did he obtain a pass?"

George sniffed. "I'll bet it was a phony—or stolen!"

Nancy was cudgeling her brain—wondering why the stranger seemed familiar. But she could arrive at no conclusion. "I guess there's nothing more we can do," she said finally.

The girls turned to gaze at the palace, built in 1128 as an abbey. The reddish-brown stone structure was still intact. It was surrounded by a large garden and a high iron picket fence.

A guide took them through the fabulous dwelling. Each room was exquisitely furnished, and the girls learned that the present royal family of Great Britain had a large apartment in the palace which they used when visiting Edinburgh.

When the girls reached the enormous, elegantly furnished dining room, Bess burst out, "Imagine eating here with your husband at one end of the table and you at the other. You couldn't even hear each other!"

The guide grinned. Then he told them a bit of Scottish history, highlighted by the final amalgamation of England and Scotland in 1603.

"This was the union of the crowns," he said, "which occurred upon the death of Queen Elizabeth I of England. At that time James VI was king of Scotland; thus he also became King James I of England."

"You mean he had both countries to run?" Bess asked, wide eyed.

"Yes. And, by the way, he had a very interesting start in life. When he was an infant, his mother had him lowered out of a high tower window in Edinburgh Castle to prevent her enemies from taking him for baptism in another faith. It was a dangerous descent."

"The poor baby!" Bess said sympathetically.

"He didn't do so badly," George remarked, "becoming king of two countries!"

Again the guide smiled, then presently escorted them back to the entrance. The girls thanked him for a most interesting tour, and a few minutes later found a taxi to take them back to their hotel. At the entrance they met Mr. Drew, who had just finished his work for the day. He and the girls went in to have tea.

The lawyer asked for an account of their day's sightseeing and frowned upon hearing about the red-bearded stranger following the girls. "If you ever see him again," he said, "I hope you can find out who he is."

"Next time I won't fail!" Nancy declared.

The lawyer reported that his conferences had been successful, but he must remain in Edinburgh a few days longer.

"I suggest that you three go on ahead of me to Douglas House. This afternoon while I was in one of the lawyer's offices I met a charming girl who comes from the Isle of Skye.

"I learned that she is about to start home and would love to catch a ride. I'm sure you girls will like her, so I invited her to have dinner with us. If you think you can all get along, she'd be glad to act as guide in Inverness-shire. Her name is Fiona Frazer, and she knows the area well."

Fiona Frazer proved to be all that Mr. Drew had prophesied. She was a beautiful girl—tall and slender, with rosy coloring, black hair, and big friendly blue eyes. After they had all met in the lobby, Fiona turned to Nancy. "Didn't I see your picture on the cover of *Photographie Internationale?*" she asked.

"Yes, I'm afraid you did. It has made me a rather conspicuous figure in your country," Nancy said, describing her recent experiences.

Fiona frowned. "Up in Inverness-shire there aren't so many people, and perhaps you won't have any trouble."

The group spent a delightful dinner hour. By the time they reached the dessert course, Nancy, Bess, and George had become very fond of Fiona. She, in turn, seemed to like them very much. It was arranged that the following morning the four girls would rent a car and start together for Douglas House.

Nancy told Fiona about the mystery they were trying to solve. "You can still change your mind about going along."

The Scottish girl laughed. "I love the sound of it and I like excitement! I'll go."

As they were eating dessert, a woman passed their table. She waved her hand graciously to Fiona and said something in a language which the girls did not understand. When the woman went on, Fiona explained, "She was speaking in Gaelic."

"What a pretty language!" said Nancy. "Do you speak it fluently?"

"Oh, yes," Fiona answered.

Nancy was intrigued. "You must teach me some words while we're driving along."

Fiona laughed. "Let's start right now." She picked up a roll from a dish which had not been removed from the table and said, "This is *aran*. It is pronounced ā-rran."

"It means bread?"

"Yes." Fiona went on, "Tomorrow we shall go on a lō-ang. It's spelled l-o-n-g, and means ship. Actually, what we're taking is a ferryboat."

Nancy blinked excitedly. She had suddenly recalled that the word *long* was in the mysterious note she had found in the bureau drawer! "Fiona, is m-a-l-l a word?" she asked.

"Yes. You pronounce it mā-ool, and it means slow."

Hearing this, Nancy opened her purse, took out her notebook, and wrote out the strange words in the mysterious note. Fiona translated:

" 'Highway ditch lock rod ship slow wife member without stamp.' Stamp means an impression."

George gave a groan. "That message is as unintelligible in English as it is in Gaelic!"

"I'm sure," said Nancy, "that the message is in code. 'Ship slow' could have meant that houseboat on Loch Lomond where the mysterious men were staying."

"You're right!" George exclaimed. "The note *was* left for Mr. Dewar. Maybe it means that if Nancy should show up, the occupants of the houseboat were to leave immediately with their possessions."

"It does look," said Mr. Drew, "as if the boxes which were removed contained stolen goods."

Nancy agreed, thinking this would tie in with her theory about a smuggling racket. Then she added grimly, "I'll bet Mr. Dewar was the driver who tried to run me off the road and cause an accident. When he failed, he went back and warned those men to get out."

Her father was thoughtful. "Nancy, if you girls are right in your theories, you have picked up one clue to many secrets that may be contained in the Gaelic code message!"

CHAPTER XI

Submerged Car

Mr. Drew and the four girls continued to stare at the strange Gaelic code message. Fiona offered a suggestion that the writer was not familiar with the language. He had merely used certain words to convey his message.

"You mean," said Bess, "that he could have done this by using a dictionary?"

"Yes."

George grinned broadly. "I was just thinking that the words 'wife member without stamp' might mean that some woman is involved in the mystery. She could be a foreigner who isn't in this country legally."

Mr. Drew looked at George admiringly. "You may have interpreted this correctly. If so, you girls had better keep your eyes open for a woman who is trying to hamper you in your endeavors."

Nancy remarked with a grin, "I can't let Bess and George get ahead of me in this guessing game! Perhaps the first two words, 'highway ditch,' meant that Mr. Dewar was to force my car into a ditch if possible."

"And he did!" Bess told Fiona.

Soon afterward, the group left the table. Fiona said good night. She would meet the girls in the morning after breakfast. "It is most kind of you to give me a ride," she said, "and I shall do my best to make the trip interesting."

At nine the following day Fiona was waiting in the lobby. Outside stood the girls' rented car, a small four-seat convertible sports model. After Nancy and her father had signed all the necessary papers, the driver went off. A porter stowed the girls' baggage in the trunk. Nancy kissed Mr. Drew good-by and took her place behind the wheel.

"We're off!" Bess cried enthusiastically. "And what a beautiful day!"

Fiona directed the way out of town and across the Firth of Forth. Then they headed northwest toward the town of Fort William.

"Are you happy to be going home to the Isle of Skye?" Bess asked the Scottish girl.

"Yes, indeed," Fiona said, smiling. "And I hope that you will be able to come and visit me before your trip is finished. I could tell you much local history and folklore."

"Tell us some now," Nancy urged. "I don't even know the names of famous spots on Skye."

"One is Borreraig, where the most famous college of piping once trained pipers from all over the Highlands!" Fiona declared, her eyes sparkling.

"A college to teach about the bagpipe?" George asked, intrigued.

"Yes, several colleges were started many centuries ago," Fiona said. "The one at Borreraig trained the MacCrimmons, a clan of fine pipers for more than two hundred years!"

"It's thrilling to think that the bagpipe we know today has such a long and colorful history," Nancy remarked as she guided the small convertible along the neat, hedge-bordered roads.

"Oh, yes, and its history is not Scottish alone," Fiona declared. "I understand the instrument first was played in Egypt as a simple chanter and drone. Later on, these were attached to a bag made of skin and fitted to a blowpipe."

"Egypt!" Bess exclaimed, then giggled. "Can you imagine King Tut playing a bagpipe?"

Fiona laughed. "Perhaps you ought to imagine that Aristotle and Julius Caesar were pipers, too, for the Greeks and Romans played the bagpipe. Then the custom spread through Europe by the Celtic and Roman invasions."

"If that's true, why do we think of it as a Scottish instrument?" George asked.

Fiona explained. "The primitive instrument is still played in isolated spots of Europe. But in most places music became an indoor entertainment and people were interested in more subdued melodies and elaborate arrangements."

"Dinner music," George suggested, and Fiona nodded.

"But its history was different in the Scottish Highlands," Fiona declared. "Our lusty people loved the martial spirit of the music of the pipes and used it for marching troops. It pepped them up when they were tired. Chiefs of the Highland clans were proud of their pipers."

"George, I wish you hadn't mentioned dinner music," Bess declared. "I'm getting hungry!"

The girls laughed, and Fiona said that they were only a short distance from an attractive golf course and hotel where they could lunch.

All the girls had healthy appetites by the time they entered the large dining room. They were intrigued by a long, flower-decorated buffet table in the center of which stood the two-foot-high statue of a golfer carved in ice.

An hour later the girls took off once more. For several more miles the drive led through wooded hillsides as well as others covered with large patches of heather. In the pastureland cattle and sheep seemed to roam at will across the road and up and down the slopes. Presently Nancy reached a long, narrow body of water which

Fiona told them was an arm of Loch Leven.

At the small village of Ballahulish, Fiona said, "We'll take a ferry from here into Invernessshire rather than drive the long way around the arm."

Nancy's car was the first to arrive at the landing. Shortly afterward, other vehicles came up and soon the ferryboat approached.

The Americans had never seen a craft like this one. It was small and flat, with a single deck. There was a tiny cabin for the pilot and his assistants at the stern. Fastened to the deck behind the cabin, and reaching to the bow of the ferry, was a turntable with stout steel raised gangplanks at either end.

Because of the strong tide, the ferry was moored alongside the pier. Slowly the turntable began to move until it was at right angles to the deck. The nearer gangplank was let down and the cars drove off. Then Nancy was waved aboard. Three cars followed and they were tightly packed in. Once more the turntable swung halfway around and the little vessel started its journey.

"Isn't this divine!" Bess remarked as the refreshing wind whipped the girls' hair.

The ride across the loch was short. When the ferry reached the opposite shore, the turntable swung around, the gangplank was lowered, and the guard motioned for Nancy to drive off. She

found herself fairly close to the edge of the cobblestone roadway which led up from the water.
There was no rail, and on either side below, a
marshy growth of reeds protruded from the surface.

"Look out!" Bess cried out.

Nancy glanced in the mirror, just in time to
see the man behind her put on a burst of speed.
The red-bearded stranger! He was so close she
could pull over only about six inches. The next
moment he gave her car a hard shove. The steering wheel twisted in Nancy's hands, and before
she could do anything, the girls' convertible shot
off into space!

All its passengers were catapulted into the
water except Nancy, who clung to the wheel and
managed to stay in her seat. The car landed upright in about four feet of water.

Immediately there were shouts of alarm. Cars
stopped and people jumped out to rush to the
girls' assistance. Completely soaked and muddy,
Bess, George, and Fiona waded to shore. Nancy,
wet to her waistline, stood up on the seat.

"I'll help you, lass!" called a man.

Already he had removed his shoes and socks
and rolled his trousers up above his knees. He
jumped into the water and quickly reached
Nancy.

She had recovered from her fright, but still

felt a little shaky as she took his hand. "This is very kind of you, sir. Thank you. I wonder how we'll get this car out."

"Ye canna drive it out, that is certain!" the Scotsman said with a smile. "But it is not a heavy car. I will fetch a group of my friends and we can lift it ashore."

"I appreciate your helpfulness," said Nancy, "but I don't want to put you to so much trouble. Isn't there a wrecker that could do it?"

"Aye, and that there be," the man replied. "If you like, I will get in touch with the owner."

Meanwhile, the other girls were fuming over the accident. "The red-bearded man caused it!" Bess declared.

At that moment a woman walked onto the dock. She gave the three girls a motherly smile and introduced herself as Mrs. Drummond.

"I am so glad you are not hurt," she said. "But I am sorry about your car. My croft home is not far from here—just beyond the mountain of Ben Nevis—and I live alone. It would be a pleasure if you lassies would stay with me until tomorrow morning. I am sure the car will not be in working condition before then."

The girls returned the woman's smile and thanked her. Bess added, "So far as I'm concerned,

I'd love to come, but first we'll have to ask our friend Nancy Drew—the poor girl out there."

The other automobiles from the ferry had begun to move. George posted herself at the pier exit and stopped each driver to ask if he knew the man who had pushed Nancy off the roadway, or had noted his license number. Neither had. They had been so horrified at the accident they had not noticed. One man did say, however, that the fellow had driven off at once.

"How dumb of me not to have spotted him on the boat!" George chided herself.

By this time Nancy had been helped ashore. "I'm all right," she assured her friends. Upon learning of Mrs. Drummond's invitation, Nancy said, "We'll be happy to accept your hospitality."

The man who had assisted Nancy then brought the girls' bags from the trunk. Fortunately the compartment was watertight, and the suitcases were only slightly damp. They were lifted up to the pier and several other men willingly carried them to shore.

Mrs. Drummond had been looking at Nancy intently. She now turned to Fiona and said something in Gaelic. Fiona smiled and told Nancy that Mrs. Drummond had asked if Nancy was the American girl detective whose picture she had seen.

Nancy laughed. "I'm surprised you recognized me in such a bedraggled condition!"

As soon as the waterlogged convertible had been towed away, Mrs. Drummond led the girls to her own car nearby. The luggage was stowed, and the five climbed in.

Mrs. Drummond's croft proved to be that in name only. The original one-room building was now the living room of a house with many other rooms. All the quaintness of the original croft had been left—its large stone fireplace, with hanging crane and iron pot; the rustic wooden chairs; the wall bed, which was now an attractive built-in sofa; and even a baby's cradle.

"Oh, this is absolutely charming!" Nancy exclaimed.

The girls were led to two bedrooms, each with a huge canopied bed and colorful hand-woven draperies and rugs. Nancy would room with Fiona.

By the time all four girls had bathed and were dressed, Mrs. Drummond had a substantial supper ready. It started with cock-a-deckie soup of leeks and a boiling hen. Then came mutton stew, filled with potatoes and small white turnips. There was kale as a side dish, and for dessert a bowl of steamed bread pudding filled with currants and topped with custard sauce.

"That was a marvelous meal!" Bess declared. "I'm stuffed!"

"But you must have a treacle doddie!" Mrs. Drummond insisted, and brought out a jar of brown sticky candy balls. Bess and her friends could not resist, and found the sweets delicious.

The girls helped Mrs. Drummond clear away the supper dishes. Then there was conversation by a cozy fire and finally the visitors said good night. Tucked under the covers at the foot of their beds each girl found an enormous hot-water bottle, which Fiona said was called a pig.

"Mm! Feels wonderful!" Nancy thought as she cuddled, giggling, down among the covers.

She slept soundly until midnight, then was awakened suddenly by the sound of bagpipes. She realized the music was some distance away, but Nancy could hear it well enough to recognize the first phrase of *Scots, Wha Hae!*

"That's funny—someone playing the pipes at this time of night—and not playing the tune very well." Instantly her mind flew to Mr. Dewar and the bagpipe playing in his hotel room.

"I'm going to find out what's going on," Nancy decided as the phrase was repeated.

She dressed quickly, tiptoed from the room, and went outside. There was a full moon, and though heavy mist lay over the landscape, Nancy was sure the music had come from a hill in the distance.

She decided to sit down on a bench near the doorway of the croft and listen. Just then she heard a truck speeding along the road toward the house. As the big closed vehicle passed by, Nancy was aware of a plaintive bleat from within, like that of a lamb.

Lambs! Sheep! Trucks! The story Ned had

told Nancy of the stealing of sheep in the Highlands of Scotland flashed into the young sleuth's mind.

Could this truck, by any chance, belong to one of the gang?

CHAPTER XII

Strange Midnight Whistle

NANCY ran forward and strained her eyes to catch the license number and make of the mysterious truck. But just then two swiftly running figures dashed up, obscuring her view.

Bess and George!

"Nancy, you scared us silly!" Bess complained. "We heard you leave your room and not come back. Why are you out here?"

The young sleuth quickly explained.

"Stolen sheep!" George exclaimed.

Just as she spoke, the girls heard a whistling sound in the distance. With intermittent stops, it continued for nearly a minute.

"What in the world is that?" Bess queried.

Nancy said she thought it was being made on bagpipes.

"I didn't know you could whistle on bagpipes," said Bess.

"I suppose you're going to tell us it's some kind of a signal!" George guessed.

"I wish I knew," Nancy said thoughtfully, and led the way back into the house.

Neither Mrs. Drummond nor Fiona had awakened, so it was not until morning that Nancy could tell about the playing of the bagpipes and the truck with a bleating lamb inside. At once Fiona said that the reed for a chanter could be split to make any kind of sound one wished. "But I don't see why anyone would want to go to the trouble of having it whistle."

Nancy did not reply but felt that there might indeed be a very good reason. If it were a sinister one, she certainly hoped to find out what it was!

Mrs. Drummond was very much concerned about the possibility of the truck having contained stolen sheep. She hurried to the telephone and called several of her neighbors to report her suspicions. When she rejoined the girls, the woman said:

"Shepherds will go out at once with their dogs to make an investigation. Perhaps you girls would like to hike around to watch."

"Indeed we would!" said Nancy. "And do you think we should notify the police?"

Mrs. Drummond said she supposed so, but added, "You know, thieves, like lightning, rarely strike in the same place twice. Besides, since we have no good description of the truck, there isn't much for the authorities to go on."

George added, "Nancy, you heard only one bleating lamb. Maybe there weren't any others inside." Nancy agreed, admitting they had no real evidence.

As soon as breakfast was over, Mrs. Drummond told the girls which direction to take to watch the shepherds and their dogs. After hiking to a hillside, they saw a shepherd dressed in clothes much like a hunter's, working with a black-and-white collie. It was rounding up sheep and bringing them to the man's side. Fiona said this was called shedding.

The Americans found it particularly fascinating to watch the strays, especially those with baby lambs. Once, an argumentative ewe was trying to keep her lamb from obeying the dog. She and her baby were pure white except for their black noses and feet. The girls laughed as the dog won out and succeeded in leading mother and daughter to the shepherd.

Bess, noticing a small daub of red paint just in front of the sheeps' tails, asked Fiona what this was for.

"It identifies the flock, which wanders all over," the Scottish girl replied. "Another farmer will use blue."

They talked for a few minutes with the shepherd, who said his dog was one of the best in the country. "He has won prizes in contests of cutting out sheep. Would you like to see him do it?" the man asked.

"Oh, yes!" the girls chorused.

He asked them to stand off at a little distance. As the collie waited, the shepherd went into the center of the assembled flock and laid his hand on the head of one of the sheep. Then he walked back to where the girls were standing.

"Trixie," he said to the dog, "bring me that sheep!"

The dog was off at once. He wound his way in and out among the animals, pushing softly at various ones and nosing at the legs of a few, to make a path for the designated sheep to get out. Now he worried the chosen ewe, which gamboled quickly to the man's side. The whole procedure had taken less than a minute!

"That's marvelous!" Nancy exclaimed.

As she stood admiring the ewe, she suddenly felt a tug on her jacket and looked down to find that the sheep had a button in its mouth! Nancy laughed and extricated it.

The shepherd grinned. "There's almost nothing a sheep won't try the taste of."

The girls thanked him for the demonstration, then hurried back to the Drummond croft. They learned from their hostess that during the night a large number of sheep had disappeared from one of the nearby farms.

"A large number?" Bess asked. "Could very many stand up in that truck you saw, Nancy?"

The young detective had a theory. "It's my guess they weren't standing up. The thieves put them to sleep, but one lamb had revived by the time I heard it. The unconscious sheep, no doubt, were piled in that truck!"

"How cruel!" Bess cried out.

Mrs. Drummond smiled ruefully. "Thieves are never kind, gentle people," she remarked. "But your idea *is* a good one, Nancy. Perhaps we should report it to the police."

"They might think my idea farfetched," said Nancy. "Let's wait until I have some concrete evidence."

At that moment the telephone rang, and after answering it, Mrs. Drummond told Nancy that her car was ready. "I'd like you girls to stay for a while, though. I'm enjoying your company. But when you're ready to go, I'll drive you to the garage."

"Thank you," said Nancy. "I think as soon as we help you tidy the house, we had better be on our way."

As the girls were about to leave, Nancy found to her embarrassment that Mrs. Drummond would not take a farthing from her guests. This proved to be the case also with the garageman. He insisted that Nancy's being pushed into the water was bad enough treatment for the visitors, and the least the natives could do for the girls was to speed them on their way without charge.

Nancy was about to insist on some kind of reimbursement when Fiona touched her arm and whispered, "Please do not say any more. These people will be offended."

Mrs. Drummond gave Nancy a little farewell squeeze and said, "If you can solve the mystery of the stolen sheep, that will be wonderful pay for all of us."

The girls climbed into the sports car, now clean and shiny, and took the road to Fort William. When they reached the attractive town with its colorful waterfront and many historic points of interest, they went sightseeing, then had luncheon at a hotel.

Afterward, Fiona took them to a museum. The girls found the quaint objects on display interesting, but what fascinated them most was a unique kind of portrait.

On a table lay a small, circular oil painting which looked like nothing else but daubs in various colors. At the center of the picture stood a cylindrical mirrored tube. When the girls looked into it, they could see the reflection of a handsome young man in Georgian clothes.

"He is our famous Bonnie Prince Charlie," Fiona explained, "grandson of King James II, and son of the Old Pretender, who lived in exile in France. In 1745 the young Charles returned to

Scotland and gathered the Highlanders under his banner. He was badly defeated at the Battle of Culloden Moor and hid out in the glens and hills.

"There were still many people in Scotland who would have liked him to win. One of these was a woman named Flora MacDonald. She had the prince disguise himself in her maid's clothes, which enabled him to escape and return to France."

"How romantic!" Bess murmured. "And oh, isn't he handsome!"

Fiona giggled. "Yes, but history tells us he did not marry until he was fifty-two."

"Better late than never," Bess said dreamily.

As the girls walked from the building, Fiona said that since the Americans were now going to Douglas House, she felt she should say good-by and go on to the Isle of Skye. Instantly Nancy, Bess, and George urged her not to leave them.

"If you're not in a hurry to get home," said Nancy, "I'd love to have you guide us around. That will be very helpful in our sleuthing."

"In that case, I'll be happy to stay with you," Fiona said. "And I should like very much to meet your great-grandmother, Nancy."

"And I want you to," Nancy replied.

Nancy's heart began to beat faster. At last she was going to meet the wonderful great-grandmother about whom she had heard so much!

CHAPTER XIII

A Surprise Announcement

THE girls traveled on a main road for some time and stopped for luncheon at a small hotel. It stood at a corner of the country road they were to follow next. The visitors were in mountainous country now, and when they set off again, Bess began to worry about the narrowness of the road.

"What do we do if a car comes the other way?" she asked, fearful that another accident would befall Nancy's automobile.

A moment later Fiona pointed to a turnout at the side of the road. "You will find many of these lay-bys on all the narrow roads in Scotland," she said.

Bess relaxed and turned her attention to the beautiful scenery. She mentioned a yellow-flowered plant which grew along the roadside. "That's lovely. What is it?"

"We call it gorse," the Scottish girl replied.

She smiled. "It blooms the year round, and there is an old saying that when gorse stops blooming, kissing will go out of fashion!"

The American girls laughed and George remarked with a twinkle in her eyes, "Bess, how about your taking home a couple of bushes to plant?"

Bess tossed her head. "What's the matter with kissing?"

About four o'clock Fiona said that she believed the grounds of Douglas House lay just ahead. The car climbed a particularly steep hill, which was flat on top. At the far end the girls could see the many chimneys of the large residence. There was an extensive area of grass and the landscape of the estate was dotted with stately sycamores, beech, and silver birch trees.

A beautiful garden surrounded the palatial home. Many flowers were already in bloom. To one side of the house was a small pond bordered by Douglas fir trees.

"What a magnificent place!" said Bess. "Nancy, I don't see why you and your father don't come here to live!"

Fiona spoke up. "It is lovely at this time of year," she said. "But it is very lonesome in winter, when the winds howl and the atmosphere is damp and cheerless."

"But *you* like it," George commented.

"When you're brought up in the Highlands,

then you do," the Scottish girl answered. "But if you are not used to the ruggedness, it can make you melancholy."

Nancy pulled up to the main entrance of the huge gray stone building. Bess, intrigued by the many small, leaded-glass windows, began to count them. She had reached thirty when the front door was opened by a man whom the girls assumed was the butler.

"I am glad you and your friends made a safe journey, Miss Drew," he said, and led the visitors through the spacious center hall into a high-ceilinged living room. "I will announce your arrival to Lady Douglas."

Even though Nancy had heard about Douglas House since her childhood, she was overwhelmed by its grandeur. On the floor were priceless Oriental rugs. The furniture was a combination of beautifully carved oak pieces and small, dainty French gilt tables and chairs.

There were two enormous, exquisitely painted Japanese lamps, and in the rear of the room was a large hanging tapestry. It depicted a scene of a young woman, dressed in a flowing robe and a bonnet, standing high on the balcony of a castle and looking at a jousting match between two knights armed with lances.

"Oh, those exciting old days!" Bess murmured.

In a few moments the butler reappeared and said Lady Douglas would see her visitors upstairs.

They followed him up the heavily carpeted stairway, which had a room-sized landing, to the second story.

Here the walls were lined with portraits in oils, apparently of deceased members of the Douglas clan. Finally the girls paused before the pleasant, elegantly furnished living room of Lady Douglas' suite. The servant stepped inside and announced them.

"Thank you, Tweedie," came a rather high but musical voice.

"So the butler's name is Tweedie!" Nancy thought. "I love it!"

She entered the room first and found herself looking upon a very slender, frail, white-haired woman with a beautiful face and of dignified mien.

Nancy made a slight curtsy and said, "Lady Douglas, I am so happy to be here."

The elderly woman arose and smiled. "No need for medieval formality, my dear," she said. "I am your great-grandmother and I would much prefer to have you call me that."

Nancy was delighted. She and her great-grandmother embraced. Nancy now turned to her friends and introduced them one by one. They were warmly welcomed and Lady Douglas said that she would be very pleased to have Fiona remain also.

"Now, let us all be seated." Lady Douglas indicated a grouping of brocaded chairs. "Morag will serve tea."

She pulled a bell cord on the wall near her, and shortly a middle-aged woman, who reminded Nancy of Hannah Gruen, appeared. She wore the conventional maid's black dress and small white apron, but the cap on her head was quite different from anything the Americans had seen. It was a frilly half-bonnet, with two long black streamers down the back.

The maid wheeled in a teacart which contained dainty, blue-flowered china, an ornate silver tea service, and several plates of tiny sandwiches and cakes.

For the next half hour the group chatted and ate the delicious food. Nancy found herself feeling that she had known her great-grandmother for years. There was an instant sense of closeness between the two.

Although eager to hear more of the missing heirloom, Nancy refrained from bringing up the subject. Finally Lady Douglas herself did so. It was apparent that the elderly woman felt Fiona, too, could be trusted with a secret, and said:

"The heirloom which Nancy was to have received was my most prized possession. It was a brooch with a large topaz in the center surrounded by diamonds."

Nancy gasped. "What a wonderful gift! It must be gorgeous!"

Her great-grandmother nodded. "The brooch was given to an ancestor of mine by Bonnie Prince Charlie."

"Oh!" Bess exclaimed. "The handsome, romantic young man who got away in a maid's disguise?"

Lady Douglas smiled. "He is the one." Then her face took on a serious expression. "Nancy, I have spent many sleepless nights since losing the pin. I last remember taking it from the safe to see if it were in proper condition to give you. The brooch appeared to be all right, and I pinned it to my dress to see how it looked.

"At that moment the room seemed a little stuffy, so I decided to go outdoors and take a walk in the garden. When I returned, it was my bedtime. I took off the dress and hung it in my wardrobe. It was not until the next morning that I thought of the brooch and decided to put it back in the safe. The pin was gone!"

"How very unfortunate!" Fiona said.

"Indeed it was," Lady Douglas agreed. "At first I thought the brooch had become unclasped and dropped off during my walk. But every part of the house and garden where I had been was thoroughly searched, and the pin was not found."

"You are sure you *lost* it?" Nancy asked.

Her relative asked wryly, "You think I might have absent-mindedly misplaced it?"

"No, Great-Grandmother dear," Nancy answered. "I wondered if it might have been stolen."

Lady Douglas looked somewhat startled. "But there was no one here except Tweedie and Morag. They are my only two servants, and both are strictly honest."

"I wasn't thinking of them," Nancy said quickly. "Perhaps your brooch did drop off outdoors, and some outsider who came here found the jewel and took it."

"That is a possibility, of course," Lady Douglas replied. "But not many people come to this lonely spot. I had a fine watchdog, but the dear creature died the very night I lost the brooch."

All this time, Nancy had been thinking of the newspaper article in the River Heights *Graphic*. She had never given up the idea that a thief or thieves had the heirloom and he had given out misleading information concerning it. But she said nothing about it.

After the tea hour was over, the visitors were shown to their rooms. Bess and George began to unpack, but Nancy and Fiona decided to go outdoors and make a search of their own. There was not a sign of the brooch, but the two girls spotted deep boot prints leading from a field at the rear of Douglas House, and back across it.

"These were certainly made by a bigger, heavier man than Tweedie," Nancy remarked.

Seeing him at work pruning some bushes, she

walked over to speak to him. He assured her that he had not made the prints and that to his knowledge no other man had been on the grounds.

"Then some stranger was here very recently, perhaps even last night, no doubt spying on the house," said Nancy. "Tweedie, do you realize that these boot marks might belong to someone who was here the night Lady Douglas lost the brooch, and that the same person might have killed your watchdog?"

The man looked startled. "Champion didn't look as if he had been hurt and we couldn't figure out what had caused his death."

Suddenly Nancy recalled her theory about the sheep thieves anesthetizing the stolen animals. Could the same method have been used on the dog, Champion, so that he could not alert those in the house?"

Another disturbing possibility occurred to Nancy. "So far the thief has taken only the brooch," she thought. "He may have come the second time to do a really big theft job!"

Nancy turned to the servant. "Tweedie," she said, *"maybe* there was a thief in the house last night. Let's find out if anything has been stolen."

CHAPTER XIV

Trouble on the Mountain

TWEEDIE raised himself proudly to his full height. "Miss Nancy, nothing could be stolen from Douglas House. Every door and window is wired to a burglar alarm. If anyone should try to sneak in, the bell would sound and the thief would soon be caught."

"I'm glad to hear that," Nancy replied, "because there are certainly some valuable pieces of furniture and silver. It is wonderful to think that sightseers from all over the world will come here and enjoy looking at the beautiful old house and grounds and the treasures inside it."

"From the first families of Scotland!" Tweedie added with pride, and walked off to continue pruning the bushes.

A few minutes later George and Bess joined the two girls. They all strolled around the grounds, at the same time reviewing the various points in the mystery. Nancy said she was convinced the brooch had been stolen.

"But by whom?" Bess asked. No one could venture a guess.

"One thing puzzles me," George declared. "If the thief who took the brooch got away safely, why would he or any of his gang try so hard to keep you from coming to Scotland, Nancy?"

"Yes, why?" Bess echoed. "Don't forget, George and I might have been killed along with you near Loch Lomond. And in the last accident— Fiona, too."

Nancy said it indicated one thing to her. "There is something bigger involved. My heirloom may be only an incidental aspect. I believe that whatever is going on actually has nothing to do with Douglas House.

"This may be a wild theory on my part, but I believe now that the same men who are stealing sheep took my brooch. They feared that if I were able to track them down, I would also uncover clues to their racket."

Fiona looked at the young sleuth admiringly. "I can see why you are an internationally known girl detective."

Bess was thoughtful. "In other words, Paul Petrie from River Heights, the mysterious Mr. Dewar, and the red-bearded man are in the sheep racket together!" Nancy nodded.

George had another thought. "Nancy, you suspected the men who moved out of that houseboat. Do you suppose the stolen brooch might have been there?"

"Maybe," said Bess, "but you couldn't hide a whole flock of sheep!" The girls laughed.

Nancy was not ready to stop talking about the mystery. "Since we suspect smuggling, wool and hides could have been hidden in the houseboat until it was time for shipment, maybe to the United States. That's where Paul Petrie might come into the picture."

"That's right!" said Fiona. "If the authorities are looking for missing live sheep, perhaps they wouldn't be looking for wool or hides."

The four girls walked along in silence for fully a minute. Then Nancy said, "Tomorrow let's take a ride to that road where I heard the bleating inside the truck."

"You mean go back to the area near Mrs. Drummond's croft?" Bess asked.

Nancy nodded and turned to Fiona. "Where could that truck have been coming from? If we go in that direction, we might pick up a clue."

Fiona said that the truck would be coming from the glen at the foot of Ben Nevis. Her face brightened in anticipation. "I have an idea. Why don't we camp out overnight? The glen is a lovely spot, popular with many mountain climbers. They even have running races up and down Ben Nevis."

George was intrigued. "How high is the mountain?"

"About forty-four hundred feet."

Bess looked aghast. "You say they *run* up?"

"That's right."

George grinned. "I want to see that place, mystery or no mystery!"

The American girls were thrilled by the idea of camping out, and later Nancy asked Lady Douglas about equipment they could use. After dinner, Nancy's great-grandmother took the girls on a tour of the mansion.

"We'll end our trip in the attic," she added, "and you girls can look there for proper hiking and camping clothes."

As the tour went on, Bess thought she had never seen such an assortment of armor and so many oil portraits in one place. There was even a knight's armor standing in a corner!

The attic was not in the least what Nancy had expected. It was very large and handsomely finished. Lady Douglas said it had once been a game room, where the men of Douglas House and their guests played billiards. Now there was the usual collection of old furniture, books, and trunks.

"You will find all sorts of clothes and blankets in the trunks," said Nancy's great-grandmother. "Help yourself to anything appropriate you can find."

The visitors were intrigued by the contents of the trunks. There were many kilt skirts, white blouses, long black socks, and various kinds of caps worn by Scottish girls.

Nancy had a sudden idea. "These would make good disguises," she said, then stopped speaking, not wishing to worry Lady Douglas with what was going through her mind. But the other girls immediately got her message.

"Let's try some on!" George urged.

To Nancy's surprise, the tartan outfits belonged to several clans, and she asked her great-grandmother about this. The elderly woman smiled. "Various relatives in our family came from different clans and brought these costumes with them."

After trying on a few combinations, Fiona chose the Ogilvy tartan of small red-and-pale-blue checks with lines of white. George's black hair was set off by the yellow-and-black plaid of the McLeods of Lewis.

Bess looked very pretty in the Stewart dress, a combination of large white squares interspersed with stripes of pale green and red.

"Nancy, I'm glad that you chose the Cameron tartan of my mother," said Lady Douglas. "It is very becoming." Nancy did look attractive in the flashy tartan of large bright-red squares edged with stripes of dark green.

"You're sure you don't mind our borrowing

these?" she asked her great-grandmother. "They may become soiled or torn on our camping trip."

Lady Douglas assured her that the costumes were not valuable and had been worn many, many times before. "I am sorry that I do not have sleeping bags or bedrolls, but in one of these trunks you will find knapsacks and warm blankets."

After the necessary equipment had been collected, the group went downstairs. Morag was told about the trip, and by the time the girls were ready to leave the following morning she had packed enough food for three good meals.

Morag admired the girls as they started off. "Aye, and ye be lookin' like bonnie Highland lassies for sure!"

The girls smilingly thanked her and said goodby. Fiona directed Nancy to drive by a shortcut to the road which went past Mrs. Drummond's croft and on to Ben Nevis. The foursome looked for any possible clues to the sheep rustlers—an encampment, or a place where a truck might have pulled off the road. They found nothing of significance.

When the girls reached the glen, they crossed a bridge over a waterfall that cascaded from a rushing, boulder-filled mountain stream.

"This scenery is gorgeous!" Bess exclaimed.

On either side mountains rose sharply but not too steeply for climbing. Rocks were interspersed with trees and bushes. Here and there grew patches of heather, its colorful purple tint giving the slope a friendly look.

The road ran alongside the water. Here and there were protected areas that Fiona said were for campers. Presently they met a group of hikers, who were about to start a race up Ben Nevis.

Nancy pulled to the side of the road and the girls got out to watch. There were four boys dressed in white trunks and jerseys with their school insigne. One boy, seeing Fiona, hailed her.

"Wish me luck!" he called. "We will run to the big pine tree. The fastest time up and back is twenty minutes."

She nodded and told the girls he was distantly related to her. The Americans were amazed at the agility and swiftness of the boys as they literally ran up the mountainside. As they neared the tree, Fiona said, "Aye, that is good. My cousin Ian is ahead!"

Ian was the first to start down the slope. This feat seemed far more dangerous than going up. By now all four girls were looking at their wristwatches. Fiona exclaimed, "I think my cousin will equal the record!"

Ian did. His time was exactly twenty minutes, while his companions were clocked at twenty-five, twenty-eight, and thirty minutes.

The Scottish girl introduced her cousin and the other boys, who immediately invited Fiona and her friends to join a group of campers up the river.

"Fiona, you know several of the girls," said Ian.

The offer was readily accepted and soon Nancy, Bess, and George were meeting Fiona's other attractive Scottish friends, most of them wearing kilts. Some campers were from the Isle of Skye and others from the town of Inverness. The Americans were made to feel at home at once.

There was a lot of chatter and laughter among the young people while they unpacked food kits. Soon everyone was eating luncheon.

Above the hum of conversation Nancy became aware of distant music. Suddenly she sat bolt upright. A few bars were being played over and over on a bagpipe, apparently somewhere far up on the mountain. The melody was *Scots, Wha Hae!*

Nancy strained her eyes to see the player, but no one was in sight. Was he just over a ridge? The young detective began to recall various incidents and finally a startling thought entered her mind. Was that particular tune, by any chance, played whenever she was around? "And could it possibly be piped by Mr. Dewar to let his partners know I'm in the area?" Nancy mused.

Her three friends had not noticed the bagpipe music, which ended abruptly. She quickly told them about it. "I'd like to climb the moun-

"The red-bearded man again!" Bess cried out

tain and look for clues to that mysterious piper!"

At once Bess said, "You might be walking right into a trap!"

Nancy smiled. "If you'll all come with me, there shouldn't be any danger."

George said practically, "That's the only way I'd let you go."

Presently the girls told the other campers where they were going and started off. The climb was hot and arduous, so there was little conversation. Nancy and Fiona forged ahead, but Bess and George did not make such good time. Finally Bess caught up. "Where's George?" Nancy asked.

Bess replied that her cousin had wanted to take a faster route to the ridge. "She wouldn't wait."

At that moment the trio heard George scream. They whirled about and gasped in horror. A short distance away on the mountainside George was just being given a hard push by the stranger who had forced their car into the water.

"The red-bearded man again!" Bess cried out.

His shove knocked George to the ground. The next moment she started rolling down the steep slope head over heels! Her assailant fled toward a shoulder of the mountaintop!

CHAPTER XV

The Phantom Piper

NANCY and Bess lost no time in scrambling after George, who was now rolling and tumbling rapidly down the mountainside.

Fortunately, a short distance below, the ground leveled off slightly. By digging in her heels, George managed to stop her descent. When the two girls reached her, Nancy asked anxiously, "Are you hurt?"

Before George could reply, Bess spoke up. "Is she hurt! Look at all those scratches! We must get you to a doctor right away, George."

"Don't be silly," George said firmly. "I feel as if I'd just had a good beating, but there's nothing more serious the matter with me."

She stood up, and with the other girls' help, brushed off as much dirt as she could.

"When we get back down, I'll have a good old cleanup in the river. Then I'll be fine." George scowled. "I'd like to catch that red-haired fellow who pushed me!"

Suddenly all three girls realized that Fiona had not followed Nancy and Bess. She was nowhere in sight, and when Nancy called there was no answer.

At once the girls became fearful. Had the red-bearded stranger tried to injure her, too?

"I'm going back up and find Fiona!" Nancy declared.

The cousins insisted upon going too, and the three hastened to the shoulder. Several times they called Fiona's name, but got no response.

Just then Nancy, standing at the highest point, saw Fiona some distance down the far slope, at the edge of a forested section. She acted as if she were trying to hide from someone.

Nancy waved the cousins on, then went toward Fiona. Reaching the Scottish girl's side, Nancy asked her what had happened.

Fiona smiled. "Maybe you're teaching me to be a detective," she said. "Anyway, I figured that since the red-bearded man was running in this direction, maybe he had come from this side of Ben Nevis. I thought I might spot him."

"Did you?" Nancy asked, as Bess and George walked up.

Fiona shook her head. "I didn't see Mr. Redbeard, but I want you all to look down there." She pointed.

In a narrow glen below them was a flock of sheep. Fiona said she had seen a shepherd there a few minutes before, but now he was gone.

"It is most unusual for any shepherd not to have a collie with him," she said. "It occurred to me that the man I saw might be an impostor, and the sheep have been stolen and brought here to await transportation."

"Fiona, you're wonderful!" Nancy cried. "This is an excellent clue and we should report it to the police."

"We can't—from here. We'll have to wait until morning."

"If Fiona's right," said Nancy, "that redbearded man has probably been following our movements very closely. Perhaps it was he who first used the bagpipe signal of *Scots, Wha Hae* to warn his friends when he found out that we were going to camp here. Then, when we were actually hiking up the mountainside and getting too near his area of operation, he had to do something desperate."

"And he thought," said George, "that if he threw me down the hill you'd all come to my rescue and give up the climb."

"Exactly."

Bess heaved a great sigh. "Since you have been alerted, Nancy, Redbeard won't dare make another move. So, for the time being, the sheep won't be taken away."

Bess's reasoning seemed sound, so the girls left the spot, made their way back to the summit, and down to the river. George bathed her face and hands in the cool water and felt refreshed.

That evening the Scottish campers entertained for the three American girls. First there was group singing of Scottish songs, old and new. Nancy and her friends were able to join in a few—"Annie Laurie," "My Luve is Like a Red, Red Rose," "The Banks o' Doon," "Sweet Afton," and "Auld Lang Syne."

After the singing was over, first the girls, then the boys put on dances to the music of bagpipes which one of the young men had brought. Then two couples danced several reels and jigs.

Presently Fiona, laughing, said to Nancy, "The next one they'll do is in your honor. It's a good jig, called 'Miss Nancy Frowned.'"

"What fun!" said Nancy, and watched closely.

Three couples performed the dance, which looked rather intricate as they went through a series of crossovers and changing of partners. Presently one of the girls dropped out and insisted that Nancy take her place. The American girl, although a good dancer, found the steps a little difficult at first. Nevertheless, the whole group clapped loudly.

The entertainment ended with a lovely solo by Fiona. Nancy, Bess, and George marveled at

her clear, birdlike voice as she sang a very pretty
tune.

"Farewell to the Highlands, farewell to the north,
The birthplace of Valour, the country of Worth;
Wherever I wander, wherever I rove,
The hills of the Highlands for ever I love."

Applause was loud. Next came a midnight
snack, then the whole group went to sleep either
under tents, in bedrolls, or wrapped in heavy
blankets.

But Nancy could not sleep. She thought the
sound of the rushing water might have a lulling
effect, but instead it seemed to be talking to her.
"I can almost hear it telling me I'm on the fringe
of a big discovery!"

About an hour later Nancy was startled to hear
a distinct whistling that she was sure came from
a bagpipe. The piper must be signaling! For
what? To whom?

Nancy crept out of her blanket, stood up, and
scanned the mountainside. The moon was already
out full, bathing Ben Nevis in a brilliant white
glow. On a ridge, some distance below the summit and partially screened by mist, Nancy saw
the silhouette of a piper. The whistling sound
had stopped and now the figure vanished.

Had the piper been a phantom or a real
person?

Nancy recalled that when she had heard the

bagpipes whistle before, the truck she suspected of carrying stolen sheep had whizzed past Mrs. Drummond's croft. Was the whistling she had just heard a signal that all was clear to move out the sheep the girls had seen in the glen?

"There's no way of my stopping them!" Nancy told herself ruefully. "Even if all we campers climbed the mountain to find out, it's so far we'd be too late."

She chafed under her helpless position, but finally sheer weariness overcame her and she dropped off to sleep.

Nancy was awake early—before anyone else. When she saw Fiona stirring a bit later, she told the Scottish girl what she had heard the night before. "Would you go up to that same shoulder of Ben Nevis with me?"

"Of course!"

When the girls reached the crest, they hurried down the other side to look down into the glen. Not one sheep was in sight!

"Oh, dear!" Fiona exclaimed. "Your hunch yesterday may have been right, Nancy."

"Let's go see if we can find any clues," Nancy urged.

On the way, Fiona remarked that Scottish flocks are allowed to wander at will around the mountainside. "So we might yet see the missing sheep."

When the girls reached the glen, there was still no sign of animals or persons around. Nancy did notice a crude, tiny croft, and thought perhaps it belonged to the shepherd.

"We'll call on him," she said.

The two walked over and knocked on the door, but there was no response. Fiona suggested that the croft might be empty, and tried the door. It was not locked. She opened it and the girls walked in. They saw a cot, a table, and a small quantity of food in a cupboard. There were ashes in the fireplace.

"Someone certainly has been staying here," Nancy remarked.

Feeling like intruders, Nancy and Fiona were about to leave when Nancy's eye was attracted to an open book on the table. She stepped closer for a second look. It was a Gaelic dictionary. Underlined on the exposed page was the word *mall!*

"Fiona, this was one of the words in that strange message in Mr. Dewar's hotel room!"

Quickly Nancy began looking through the dictionary for other words in the message.

"Here's rathad!" she said excitedly. "It's underlined too!"

Next she found *dig, glas, slat, long, bean, ball, gun, ail.* All had been marked!

CHAPTER XVI

Charge Against Nancy

Iт took both Nancy and Fiona a few moments to realize what a great discovery they had made. Then the Scottish girl asked, "Will you tell all this to the police?"

"Yes, indeed, and also what happened at Mrs. Drummond's." Nancy's brow furrowed in concentration. "Fiona, I wonder if the words 'highway ditch' in the message could mean a particular road on which the thieves travel."

Fiona looked surprised. "I thought you had decided it meant Mr. Dewar or one of his friends was to force your car into the ditch."

"That was only a guess. And my new theory is too. I wish I could decipher 'lock rod' and 'wife member without stamp.' "

Nancy decided to leave the dictionary open at the page bearing the word *mall* so as not to alert the person staying in the cabin that anyone had been there. Nancy picked up the book to turn the pages and suddenly gasped.

Underneath it lay a paper with her autograph!

"What's the matter?" Fiona asked.

Nancy explained and her Scottish friend looked worried. "Then the man who bought your autograph from the little boy in River Heights is using this croft as a hideout."

Nancy was in a quandary. Although pieces of the puzzle were beginning to fall into place, she was now doubly worried about her involvement in the mystery. "I'm positive now that Paul Petrie or someone working with him has my autograph to use for an illegal purpose."

Again Nancy's thoughts flew to the word "wife" in the strange message. Was somebody's wife impersonating Nancy and using her signature?

The young sleuth wondered what to do. If she removed the piece of paper, the occupant of the croft would be put on guard and might run away and warn his friends to vanish also.

"This is too good a chance to miss for the authorities to capture one of the men red-handed," Nancy decided. "I'll leave the paper."

She replaced it on the table and covered the autograph with the open dictionary. Before leaving the croft, the two girls peered cautiously outside. No one was in sight, so they hastened up the slope and down the other side to the river. All the campers were awake and breakfast preparations were under way.

"Nancy! Fiona!" cried Bess and George together, when the two appeared. Bess added, "Where have you been? Everybody has been looking for you!"

"I'm sorry," said Nancy.

She quickly whispered her exciting news to the cousins. They were astounded and glad to start back for Douglas House directly after breakfast.

When they reached the estate, the girls found Lady Douglas walking in the garden. She was surprised at their early return and exclaimed, "Don't tell me you have solved the mystery!"

"No, Great-Grandmother," Nancy replied. "But we think we have a valuable clue. I want to report to the police immediately."

Lady Douglas' face clouded. "The police want to speak with you also, Nancy. I'm afraid I have disturbing news for you."

The elderly woman said that a telephone call had come from the local superintendent. "When they told me why they wanted to get in touch with you, I said the whole thing was utterly preposterous. The very idea of their being suspicious of you!"

Nancy took her great-grandmother's arm and said, "They are suspicious of *me!* What about?"

Lady Douglas explained that recently a number of worthless checks for large amounts had been cashed in Scotland. The signature had been traced to the girl whose picture was on the cover of *Photographie Internationale*.

Nancy's face was grim. "So my autograph *has* been dishonestly used—by a forger!"

She now told Lady Douglas about the man who had purchased her signature from the little boy and how she had found it in the croft.

"This is more serious than I thought," said Lady Douglas. "I told the superintendent he had no right even to mention this to you, but he was insistent, so I finally promised him you would call the office as soon as you arrived and explain the matter yourself."

"Excuse me, please," said Nancy, and ran into the house.

Her phone call was answered by the superintendent, who said he would send Inspector Anderson and Inspector Buchanan to the mansion to talk to her. By the time they arrived, Lady Douglas and the four girls had assembled in the big drawing room.

Anderson was young, very pleasant, and appeared to believe Nancy's denial that she had written any worthless checks. His fellow officer, however, was a bit gruff. It was clear that Buchanan thought Nancy was not telling the truth, mainly because the evidence against her was so overwhelming.

"I have no accounts in this country," said Nancy, "so naturally I have no checks. The guilty person perhaps only resembles me slightly."

"On the contrary," Buchanan said brusquely, "we have an accurate description of the young woman and it fits you. Also, several people have identified the photograph on the magazine cover as being that of the person who cheated them."

Nancy was stunned. As she was trying to figure out what to say next, Buchanan told the girls he had orders for none of them to leave the house until they had permission from the police office.

Lady Douglas spoke for the first time. "If I say I will take full responsibility for Miss Drew and her friends, will that satisfy your superintendent?"

Nancy realized that the situation had reached a ticklish stage. Buchanan obviously did not wish to risk incurring the displeasure of Lady Douglas. On the other hand, he had his duty to perform. The young sleuth had a sudden inspiration—she would try to reach her father on the telephone and see if he could settle the matter!

She put the question to the two inspectors and they agreed. Fortunately, Nancy was able to locate the lawyer in his Edinburgh hotel room. When he heard the story, Mr. Drew became angry and insisted upon talking to one of the inspectors.

Buchanan came to the phone, and after a few

minutes' conversation with the lawyer he hung up and in turn telephoned his superior. Nancy rejoined the others in the drawing room.

Finally Buchanan returned and announced, "Mr. Drew also has offered to take full responsibility for his daughter's appearance in court if required. For this reason, you young ladies will not have to stay on the premises."

"Thank you," said Nancy. "I'm going to try tracking down the person who's using my name on worthless checks!" She thought she had a couple of good leads, but did not divulge these to the inspectors.

Nancy did tell them, however, about the sheep-stealing incident at Mrs. Drummond's and of her suspicion that the croft in the glen might be a hideout of one of the sheep thieves. "Yesterday I saw a flock there, but every animal was gone early this morning. If you go to the croft, you will find my name on a piece of paper. It was left by someone who obtained my autograph in the United States."

The two officers looked at Nancy in astonishment. She thought she detected a more conciliatory expression in Buchanan's eyes. Nancy added, "You will find the autograph under a Gaelic-English dictionary."

The inspectors went off, saying the glen would be investigated at once. After luncheon Nancy telephoned the police office to find out if there were any news yet.

"Yes, Miss Drew. Everything had been removed from the croft but the furniture."

Nancy's heart sank. Another good lead had ended in failure!

"What about the sheep?" she asked. "Did you learn whether or not they had been stolen?"

"We did. A farmer has reported about fifty missing. He said they vanished like the little people of Fairy Bridge."

When Nancy returned to the other girls, she reported the latest news, then asked Fiona, "What did the man mean by the little people of Fairy Bridge?"

The girl from Skye gave Nancy a whimsical look. "There is a legend that long ago a race of people, like sprites or Welsh leprechauns, lived not far from my home. They loved to play tricks, but when the giants—the big people—came around, the little people knew they could not cope with them. They always hid until it was safe for them to come out and cause some more innocent devilry. One of their hiding places was under a very ancient stone bridge which came to be known as the Fairy Bridge."

Nancy and her friends smiled, and Bess said with a sigh, "I wish we would meet charming characters like that nowadays instead of sheep and jewel thieves!"

The girls walked around the garden, all chattering gaily except Nancy. Finally George said to her, "What's on your mind, Nancy? I'll bet you want to go back to that croft in the glen and do a little sleuthing yourself. But you're afraid the police won't approve."

"You've guessed it!"

"Let's go, anyhow!" George urged.

Nancy said with a rueful grin, "I've had enough trouble with the police, but I'll go if my great-grandmother gives her consent."

To her delight, Lady Douglas approved of the idea, saying, "I realize how real a detective you are, Nancy, and that you have three incentives— finding your missing heirloom, the sheep thieves, and now the worthless check passer. I know you feel the three mysteries are intertwined." She kissed each of the girls in turn. "Best of luck to you all!"

Fiona thought she could find a shortcut to the side of the mountain where they had seen the hidden glen. At her direction Nancy turned the car off the main road and onto a very lonely one. Presently the girls became aware of billowing smoke in the distance. As they rounded a bend they were startled to come upon a hillside of dry seedlings on fire.

At once Fiona cried out, "We must get the brooms and beat it out!"

CHAPTER XVII

The Chase

"BROOMS?" Bess echoed. "What do you mean, Fiona?"

"You will see. Nancy, speed up! We must put out the fire before it spreads to the tall trees!"

Nancy did not stop for questions. She raced the car along the road until Fiona said, "Slow down! The brooms are right ahead!"

At the edge of the field was a wooden stand containing stout brooms. Nancy pulled over. Fiona hopped out and dashed to grab four of them. As she rejoined the others, the Scottish girl said the brooms were made of birch twigs, bound together with stout wire. "These are always kept handy for fire fighting."

Nancy quickly backed the car around and sped off. Fiona explained that anyone who spotted a brush fire was supposed to try putting it out. A few seconds later Nancy reached the scene of the burning seedlings.

"We'll separate and work on the outer edges," Fiona ordered. "It may feel a little hot on your feet, but we can't do anything about that."

The girls wielded the brooms vigorously on the burning hillside and within half an hour they had extinguished the centermost point of the blaze. The young fire fighters leaned on their brooms wearily. They had saved the big trees!

"I'm sure glad that's over!" said Bess. She would have liked to sit down and rest, but there was no place to do this.

As the foursome trudged back to the road, they looked at one another. The girls' faces were red and perspiring from the heat. Their hands were rough and beginning to show a few small blisters. Skirts and sweaters were dirty and the color of their shoes unrecognizable.

George remarked, "We're sure a sorry sight! I hope we don't meet anybody."

Bess giggled. "You spoke too soon. Look who's waiting for us!"

A car had stopped behind Nancy's and two police officers were standing in the road.

"Anderson and Buchanan!" George exclaimed.

When the girls, carrying their brooms, reached the roadway, the two men looked at them in astonishment. Nancy spoke up, giving Fiona all the credit for knowing what to do.

"But the main thing is, you succeeded!" Buchanan said admiringly.

"I'm glad we were here at just the right moment," said Nancy, and started toward her car.

Inspector Buchanan hesitated a moment, then walked up to her. "I'm sorry, Miss Drew, that I ever had any doubts about your honesty. I'm sure that no check forger would take time to stop and put out a forest fire."

Nancy smiled at him. "You were only doing your duty," she said. "Let's forget the whole thing, shall we?"

Buchanan nodded and his companion grinned.

Nancy and her friends climbed into the car and waved to the two men. Nancy drove off, leaving Anderson and Buchanan to make a final check of the fire scene.

In a little while the girls reached a spot where Fiona suggested they park.

"We'll climb from here. I think I can find that glen with the croft where we saw the sheep."

The Scottish girl proved to be a good pathfinder and presently located a trail leading up the mountainside. Nancy figured that this probably was the route along which the stolen sheep were driven, then anesthetized and piled into a waiting truck.

The girls kept a sharp lookout but saw no one. A few minutes later they reached the croft and began a search of the premises. Not a single clue came to light.

"The only place we haven't looked," George said, "is in that heap of ashes in the dooryard."

She and Bess found long twigs and began to scatter the ashes. Underneath was a heap of unburned trash. It contained tin cans, banana peels, and bits of broken glass.

"That phony shepherd who lived here was a good housekeeper, anyway!" said Bess. "He certainly tidied up this place."

The remark intrigued Nancy. She wondered why, if the man had intended to get away in a great hurry, he should have bothered to clean up.

Bess was still delving and presently found a small canvas nailed to a board. On it was a conglomeration of colored paints. "What in the world is this?" she asked. After looking at it a moment, she tossed the canvas aside.

Nancy picked it up. Since it was so foreign to the rest of the debris, she felt it might have some significance. No explanation came to her at the moment, so she decided to take the canvas along.

The pile of rubbish was again put together and the ashes sprinkled over the top. Nancy said she thought it was time to call a halt to the investigation.

"Let's go home now."

During the ride back, Nancy was quiet and

thoughtful. By the time they reached Douglas House, she had decided to try an experiment. After bathing and dressing, she went on a search and collected several hand mirrors.

Later Fiona, Bess, and George found Nancy in Lady Douglas' sitting room with her great-grandmother. The young sleuth was bending over a table. On it she had laid the canvas, with the mirrors propped up in a circle in the middle of it.

"What on earth are you doing, Nancy?" Bess demanded.

"I had a hunch," her friend replied. "This canvas, which has various colors that don't seem to depict anything, may have been painted like the picture we saw of Bonnie Prince Charlie in the museum. Remember? The one with the cylindrical mirror in the center which reflects the portrait of the prince?"

The other girls nodded and peered into the mirrors. None of them could see anything like a picture. Lady Douglas examined the canvas, but could make nothing out of it.

"I agree with Nancy, though, that this might have some significance," she said. "But how else can we try to find out?"

"Perhaps we have the wrong arrangement," said Nancy. "Have you a circular glass object which I could make into a mirror?"

Lady Douglas said she could not think of anything, but Nancy was welcome to look around the house and use whatever she could find.

At once the young detective set off with the canvas. In a cupboard on the first floor she found a large goblet of clear glass.

"Just the right size," Nancy decided. "I hope my idea works."

She returned to her great-grandmother and asked if it would be all right to paint quicksilver on the inside of the goblet to make it serve as a mirror.

"Yes, indeed, Nancy. Perhaps Tweedie can help you. He has all sorts of things cached away, and possibly may have some quicksilver."

Unfortunately Tweedie had none, so Nancy decided to drive into Fort William and purchase a small quantity of the coating.

The other girls wanted to go along, so presently the foursome was on its way. As they turned into the main street, Nancy said excitedly, "Look! Isn't that the red-bearded stranger in the car up ahead?"

Her friends followed her glance. "Sure is!" George declared grimly. "He's in a different car."

Nancy set her jaw. This time he was not going to get away from her! She memorized the license number of his car and then set out in pursuit.

The man was driving fast and Nancy increased her own speed. For a few minutes she was afraid she might be stopped by some constable. But presently both cars were out of town and the chase continued.

The red-bearded man seemed to know that he was being followed. He put on a tremendous burst of speed and raced down the road. Nancy kept right after him!

The pursuit went on and on, southward, in the general direction of Loch Lomond.

"Maybe he's going to the houseboat!" Bess suggested when they were halfway there.

George said she hoped he would stop there. "It'll give me great pleasure to nab him and turn him over to the police!"

Nancy took her eyes off the road for one second to look at her gas gauge. It registered empty!

"Oh, dear!" she exclaimed in dismay. "I'll have to stop for gas, and we'll lose our man!"

CHAPTER XVIII

Unmasked

THE words were hardly out of Nancy's mouth when her car coughed and came to a halt. She groaned.

George shrugged in resignation. "Well, that's that! Anyway, Nancy, you can't blame *this* car trouble on your unknown threateners!"

Nancy did not answer. She slipped from the car and ran up the road to a house. A pleasant-looking woman answered her knock.

As Nancy asked, "May I use your phone? I want to call the police," the woman stared at her.

Finally she smiled and said, "You're the American girl detective, aren't you? The one whose picture I saw on the cover of *Photographie Internationale!*"

"For once I'm glad to be recognized," said Nancy, smiling.

The woman invited Nancy inside and motioned to a telephone on the hall table. Nancy asked her how to get the proper police office and soon was connected with the superintendent.

"Yes, lass?"

Nancy quickly reported that she was on the trail of a red-bearded man who, she thought, was a sheep thief. "Inspectors Anderson and Buchanan know me," she added.

"Your story is very interesting," said the police officer, who told her his name was MacNab.

Nancy explained how the suspect had eluded her. "Please, won't you try to apprehend him?" She gave the license number of his car. "If you catch the man, will you hold him at headquarters until I can come and identify him?"

Mr. MacNab promised to follow her suggestion. "Perhaps you had better come here, anyway. I'd like to hear more of your story."

Nancy assured him she would be there shortly, then, after receiving directions to police headquarters, said good-by. She next asked the kind woman, who said she was Mrs. Evans, how to telephone for petrol and this time was relieved of the chore by her accommodating hostess.

While they were waiting for the petrol to arrive, Mrs. Evans asked curiously about the red-bearded stranger Nancy was chasing. "Is he involved with some case you're working on?"

Nancy answered as offhandedly as she could. "I'm staying at my great-grandmother's outside of Fort William. As you may know, a good many sheep have been stolen from that area. I just happened to pick up a clue that might connect this man with the thieves. I thought it was worth reporting."

The young detective's explanation seemed to satisfy Mrs. Evans, who switched the conversation to Nancy's great-grandmother. "I learned from the papers that you were going to visit Lady Douglas."

Nancy laughed. "You may be interested to know also that a friend of mine entered my photograph in a contest and won a trip for two people. Those two are out in the car right now, and I must return to them." Nancy opened her purse. "How much do I owe you for the phone calls?"

Mrs. Evans looked surprised. "Why, my dear lass, I would not think of taking any money. It has been very delightful to meet you and to be of service. It's funny how people's paths cross, isn't it? In this case, an empty petrol tank brought you to me!"

She broke into a jolly laugh and accompanied Nancy to the car. At that moment a serviceman pulled up with a large container of petrol and poured the petrol into the tank. In the meantime, Nancy had introduced her friends to Mrs. Evans. Then, after paying the garageman, she thanked Mrs. Evans for her kindness and drove off.

When George noticed that Nancy did not turn around in the direction of Douglas House, she asked where they were going. Nancy grinned. "To the police office!"

When the girls entered the building, they could have cried out for joy. Their quarry had been apprehended! He was standing in front of Superintendent MacNab's desk, declaring loudly, in a manner of speech which proclaimed him to be an American, that he was innocent.

"Sure as I'm Sandy Duff, I'll make it hot for you if you don't let me out of here!"

Bess, George, and Fiona took seats in the rear of the room as Nancy walked forward. Peering over the prisoner's head, Mr. MacNab asked, "You are Miss Nancy Drew?"

At this, Sandy Duff wheeled and faced the girl detective. His face went white. The officer said, "I believe you know who Miss Drew is?"

Sandy Duff's arrogance quickly returned. "I never saw her in my life!" he shouted.

At that moment a constable walked into the room. George hurried over to him and said in a low tone, "I think the prisoner is wearing false hair and whiskers."

The constable smiled. He did not reply, but went up and whispered in Mr. MacNab's ear.

"Aye? We shall soon see!"

His superior immediately ordered the constable to find out if the prisoner was wearing a wig. Sandy Duff objected strenuously, but to no avail. In a moment the officer was holding a red wig in his hands. The prisoner's own hair was black! Next, the side whiskers and beard were pulled off.

Nancy was amazed. She cried out, "He's Paul Petrie, from my home town!"

The excitement brought the other girls forward and everyone talked at once until the superintendent rapped for silence. He said, "Miss Drew, please tell us your story."

Nancy started at the beginning, when the stranger, whom she learned later was named Paul Petrie, had purchased her autograph from a small boy. "I got a good look at Mr. Petrie at that time. That's probably why I thought he seemed vaguely familiar when he followed me in Edinburgh. But that time, of course, he was wearing his disguise."

The girl detective explained that she had come to Scotland hoping to trace an heirloom which she now suspected had been stolen by Paul Petrie or one of his associates.

"I didn't do it!" the prisoner snarled.

Nancy paid no attention. She went on to relate how the sheep-stealing racket had come to her attention and that through having seen a secret code message she had traced the thieves first to a houseboat and then to a croft on Ben Nevis.

Paul Petrie's face was livid. "I don't know what you're talking about!"

Nancy turned to Mr. MacNab. "One thing Mr. Petrie cannot deny is having my autograph in his possession. I suspect that the wife of one of the men in Petrie's group is responsible for forging my name on checks. She herself may look like me or, if not, has been able to disguise herself in such a way that if questioned she could produce the magazine cover with my picture and carry out her scheme."

The superintendent looked sternly at the prisoner. "What have you to say to this charge?"

"Nothing. There's not a word of truth in any of it. I'm not Paul Petrie and I demand to be released." He had no identification on him to prove who he was.

The police officer said he thought the evidence was strong enough against the man to warrant holding him without bail until the police had a chance to investigate his story and also that of Nancy Drew.

After the suspect had been led away, Mr. MacNab asked the young sleuth many more questions. He ended by saying, "You have done an excellent bit of detective work, Miss Drew."

Praise embarrassed Nancy. Blushing, she said, "May I use your telephone? My friends and I were making a hurried trip into Fort William, and I know Lady Douglas expected us back soon. I am afraid she will be worried."

"Aye, of course," the officer said.

Nancy's great-grandmother was so startled by the latest news that Nancy told her they would start home at once. But just as the girls were about to leave, the constable who had placed Petrie in a cell caught up to them. "The prisoner wants to make a bargain with you lassies," he said.

"What is it?" Nancy asked.

"I do not know."

The superintendent was informed of Petrie's offer and said he himself would go to the cell with the girls and find out what the man meant. Petrie looked pleased when they arrived.

"Like I told you before, I'm not guilty of doing anything wrong," he said, "but I do know where that missing heirloom is. If you'll let me go, I'll tell you."

The astounded girls turned to Mr. MacNab. After all, it was his decision to make.

He replied firmly, "I certainly cannot release you at this time. But if you will reveal what you know about the missing heirloom, things may go easier for you."

Paul Petrie shrugged. "Okay. Miss Drew, that man Tweedie at Lady Douglas' house has the heirloom!"

CHAPTER XIX

The Enemy Spotted

"TWEEDIE!" Bess exclaimed, aghast. *"He* couldn't have taken Nancy's heirloom!"

Paul Petrie smirked. "You think that butler is honest, but you'll find out to the contrary when you investigate."

Nancy and her friends were thunderstruck by Petrie's accusation. All were skeptical, but had to admit they knew little about the servant.

"We'd better get back and find out!" said George.

Nancy thought so too. The girls left the police office and hurried to their car. Nancy drove at a fast speed all the way to Fort William. Fiona hopped out of the car long enough to buy a bottle of quicksilver and a paintbrush, then the ride was continued.

As soon as they reached home, the four girls rushed to Lady Douglas' suite and told her what they had heard.

"It cannot be true!" she said. "Tweedie has been here many, many years, and I have never had any reason to doubt his honesty."

Nevertheless, she felt that she should question the man. Unsuspecting of what he was about to hear, Tweedie smiled pleasantly when he appeared and asked Lady Douglas what she wished.

"I am at a loss for words," said Nancy's great-grandmother, "but I feel I must find out something from you. A report has come to us that you have the topaz-and-diamond brooch meant for Miss Nancy."

Tweedie went ash white and began to tremble. For several seconds he was speechless. Nancy felt sorry for the man and longed to help him, but she knew that this was Lady Douglas' affair.

By now Tweedie had recovered his wits. "Lady Douglas," he said with dignity, "I did not take the brooch. I know nothing about the pin. It is my belief that whoever accused me is covering up something himself."

Lady Douglas smiled at her long-time servant. "I was sure this would be your reply. I never doubted you."

Nancy now told Tweedie of having caught an American who, she believed, was in league with the sheep stealers. "I have a hunch that when the police obtain a confession from him and his friends, we will also get a clue to the missing heirloom."

To show she had complete confidence in him, Nancy asked Tweedie if he would help her make a mirror out of a goblet. The man looked surprised, but when told that it might aid in producing a clue in the mystery, he was eager to help. In a short time the quicksilver had dried and the cylindrical mirror was ready to be put to use.

Lady Douglas, Tweedie, and the other girls were interested onlookers as Nancy placed the goblet mirror upside down in the center of the canvas board containing the conglomerate of paint. This time, Nancy could distinguish a tower of stones.

"Have you any idea what this could be?" she asked her great-grandmother.

After a little study, both Lady Douglas and Tweedie thought that the tower might be part of ancient stone ruins not far away.

"It is in a deserted area," said Tweedie. "Would you like me to guide you girls there?"

"Oh, yes!" Nancy replied. "Since we found this picture where we know one of the sheep thieves was staying, I'm sure it has something to do with their work—it might even indicate another hideout!"

Plans were made for a trip early the following day. The girls learned that the ruins were called beehives because of their shape. They were also known as brochs, and dated back to prehistoric times.

Soon after breakfast the next morning the searchers set out. Tweedie directed Nancy onto a narrow, little-used country road and twenty minutes later the visitors got their first glimpse of the stone tower.

"It really is shaped like a beehive," Bess remarked, "except it has no top."

Nancy parked, and Tweedie led the girls across a meadow to view the ruins. The odd structure had no windows. It was made of varied sizes of fieldstones and stood about thirty feet high.

Tweedie said, "It must have been much higher at one time, and perfectly round. Only the front section is standing now."

He led the way to a very narrow opening—the only one into the broch. The passage was barely two feet wide, and tunneled through the ten-foot-thick wall.

"This is an amazing sight," Nancy remarked, looking at the circular, upcurving stonework.

At intervals there were oblong openings with stone slabs laid crosswise in them like floors.

"What were those little rooms used for?" Bess asked.

Tweedie replied that historians were not sure. Some thought that during times of enemy invasions, an entire village of people would crowd into the broch, seal off the entranceway, and live there until the danger was over.

"Probably a whole family lived in one of those rooms," Tweedie continued. "Originally there was a circular staircase with a gallery at each level which permitted the inhabitants to go up and down. Also, they had a large hearth in the center for cooking. Now, I'll show you something else."

He led the girls around a low wall that was still standing and pointed out an entrance to a lower level. "That was where they had a well and got their water."

George asked, "If the beehive was solid—how did those people get any air?"

Tweedie said that most scholars felt the top was open and ventilation was provided through a latticed roof with a veranda. "Some archaeologists even believe this was used as a living room."

"Very cozy," Bess commented. "But I'd still prefer hotel accommodations!"

The others laughed. Then Nancy's thoughts turned to the mystery they were trying to solve. The girls looked around for clues but found none.

"There's certainly no sign of anyone's hiding out here," Nancy said finally.

Fiona turned to Tweedie. "Isn't there another broch up the road a ways?"

When he said Yes, Nancy urged that they go to

see it. They reached this beehive a few minutes later and began investigating. Suddenly the young sleuth said excitedly, "Here are some bits of wool! And a piece of sheepskin!"

"You think the sheep thieves use this place?" Fiona asked.

"Yes," said Nancy. "And this evidence indicates they are not taking away live sheep to butcher or sell. They want only the wool and skins."

Bess groaned in distaste. "Ugh!" she said. "You mean the area around this broch might be a sheep graveyard?"

Nancy did not reply. She noticed that Tweedie had slipped away. She felt sure he was doing some investigating on his own, which proved to be true. He came back a few minutes later and announced that he had done a little digging with a sharp stone.

"I'm afraid this is indeed a sheep graveyard."

The group was able to piece the whole operation together now. Apparently the thieves lured a flock into some hidden glen, put them to sleep, and transported them by truck to this broch. Here they killed the sheep, sheared and skinned them, took the meat, then buried the rest to avoid detection by the police.

"I think we should return to Douglas House at once," said Nancy, "and inform the police office of our latest findings."

They sped back to the house and Nancy put in the call. After hearing the story, the officer promised to post men at the broch and try to catch the thieves red-handed.

"I will let you know as soon as we have any news," he promised.

The next day the girls attended church services and awaited word from the police. It was not until the following morning that the superintendent telephoned to say that nothing suspicious had happened at the broch.

"But down at Dumbarton on the Clyde," he added, "inspectors have come upon an illegal shipment of wool and sheepskins aboard a freighter destined for the United States."

After the call was ended, Nancy said to the other girls, "Dumbarton is directly south of where the houseboat stood on Loch Lomond. I'll bet that's the place Paul Petrie was heading for when we were chasing him."

George spoke up. "But Dewar and the other thieves weren't caught there. Where are they?"

Nancy shrugged. "They're not at the croft, not at the houseboat, and not at the broch. They're holed up somewhere, and it's my idea that they're waiting for a signal."

"From whom?" Fiona asked.

"Paul Petrie!"

The others were startled but could see the logic of Nancy's deduction. Bess and George recalled the bagpipe music in Mr. Dewar's room. "It could have been Petrie practicing," George said. "Then there was the piper on Ben Nevis who played the very same tune."

"I've just had a brainstorm," Nancy declared. "Great-Grandmother, it's a daring one, but I hope you won't have any objections. I'd like to dress in the Cameron kilt and the rest of the costume I wore before, climb Ben Nevis to the point where I saw that piper, and play *Scots, Wha Hae.*"

"You can play that on the bagpipes?" Lady Douglas asked in amazement.

Nancy confessed that she could render only the first few bars on the chanter, but they were all the mysterious piper had played. She would use the full instrument, however, to imitate him. She went on to explain about the whistling on the bagpipes, which was apparently the second signal used by the gang.

"I'll need a chanter that can produce a whistle," Nancy told her relative. "Can you help me obtain one?"

Lady Douglas was intrigued by the scheme. She said, "Tweedie was once a reedmaker in a factory. In fact, he has several bagpipes, although he can't play. I'll ask him to bring them." She pulled the bell cord.

In a few minutes Tweedie appeared. He was surprised at Lady Douglas' request, but was glad to assist. He invited the whole group to his own little sitting room and workshop where he kept his bagpipes.

"They are all in working order," he said proudly, and invited Nancy to try them.

She did, and found one which was not so heavy to carry as the others. After playing the first phrase of *Scots, Wha Hae* several times she did it like a professional.

"Could you make me a reed that whistles and put it into a chanter?" Nancy asked Tweedie.

"Aye, and that I could," he replied. "I can have it ready in an hour. Will that be all right?"

Nancy said she would like to use it that evening, and since it stayed light so late, there was no hurry.

As Lady Douglas and the girls went back to her sitting room, Bess said, "Now, Nancy, tell us your whole idea."

The young detective smiled. "I thought we four girls could go to Ben Nevis glen this evening and camp out. Near sunset I'll climb the mountain to the spot where I saw the piper, and play the two signals. If the thieves are in the area—and I have a hunch they are—my signaling may start something."

"It sounds fine," said Bess, "but I think we should take a couple of police officers with us for safety."

Lady Douglas agreed. She herself telephoned

the superintendent, who said he would send two men up in the early evening. Nancy was delighted later when Tweedie handed her a chanter containing the new reed. She practiced on it until she could obtain a good strong whistle.

The officers who arrived at Douglas House were Anderson and Buchanan! Both carried binoculars.

Morag had packed a picnic supper and the group set off in two cars. Soon after reaching the campsite they ate, and for a while sat around discussing the mystery. When the light began to wane, the group started up the mountain.

Anderson was carrying Nancy's bagpipes and talking with her animatedly in low tones. Bess giggled and whispered to George, "Ned Nickerson ought to see her now! Bet he'd be jealous."

About halfway to their goal, Nancy heard a stealthy sound to her left beyond some boulders and trees. She darted off by herself to investigate. On the far side of a thicket she saw a lone lamb which started to bleat pitifully. Nancy walked over to comfort the baby animal.

Suddenly she felt the presence of something behind her and turned to look. Poised on the limb of a nearby tree, and about to spring toward her and the lamb, was a large wildcat!

CHAPTER XX

Detective Divers

For a moment Nancy panicked. Would the wildcat pounce on her for interfering with his intent to attack the lamb?

A sudden thought came to Nancy. She had once heard that yelling loudly and heaving stones could scare off a wildcat. Though she knew it might ruin her chances of tricking the sheep thieves by alerting them, she had to take that risk.

Nancy, at the top of her lungs, shouted repeatedly, *"Scat! Get out of here!"* She kept hunting for a stone, found a good-sized one a moment later, and threw it at the hissing animal.

The wildcat leaped off the branch to keep from being hit but did not attack. Apparently frightened, the beast turned tail and ran off!

Nancy, weak with relief, sat down beside the baby lamb. She gave her a hug and said, "You go

Nancy shouted at the top of her lungs

find your mother! Run, now!" She gave the animal a gentle slap and watched her start down the mountainside.

The commotion had brought Bess, George, and the two inspectors on the run. Nancy told them what had happened, and said she hoped her scheme for bringing the thieves into the open had not been ruined.

"We must take that chance," said Anderson. "I'm glad you weren't mauled."

Nancy felt encouraged. "Let's go!" she said.

As soon as they reached the ridge, Anderson handed her the bagpipes. Nancy stood alone on a little promontory, while the others remained hidden. She played the first phrase of *Scots, Wha Hae* loudly and clearly.

In the meantime, the two inspectors had trained their binoculars on the landscape. Far below, in a natural hollow, stood a flock of sheep. Four shepherds were tending them.

Buchanan handed his binoculars to Bess and asked if she could identify any of the men. It was fully a minute before she could get a good look at their faces. Suddenly she said excitedly, "One of them is Mr. Dewar!"

Just then, Anderson, through his glasses, spotted a large, covered truck parked on the nearby country road. The vehicle was well screened by trees.

Inspector Anderson said, "Mr. Buchanan and

I will circle around to that spot and watch what's going on. You girls wait here. Give us twenty minutes, Miss Drew, and then play the whistling sound on your bagpipes."

George said, "May we borrow the binoculars so *we* can see what's going on?"

Anderson laughed as he turned his over to her. "Aye, and I don't blame you for wanting to watch."

The two inspectors scrambled down the mountainside. Nancy changed the chanter on the bagpipes and then kept her eyes on her wristwatch, while George trained the binoculars on the flock of sheep.

"Here goes!" said Nancy finally.

Putting the mouthpiece to her lips, she made a whistling sound. It was exactly the same as the one she had heard several times before.

Within a few seconds George began to report what she was seeing through the binoculars. "Those four men have some kind of guns and are spraying the sheep!"

Nancy, Bess, and Fiona could vaguely make out the scene below and were horrified a minute later to see the animals toppling over.

The men dragged the motionless sheep one by one to the rear of the truck. Finally the van was filled, and the thieves drove off.

The girls were speechless until Bess burst out, "Why didn't the inspectors stop them?"

"Perhaps," said Nancy, "they're going to follow those men to get more evidence." As the
truck pulled out of sight, she added, "Let's go
back to Douglas House and wait for word from
the police."

When they arrived, Nancy's great-grandmother
was relieved to see them. She was astounded at
the girls' story, and said, "My congratulations!"

Nancy smiled. "Let's not celebrate until the
case is ended. I still must locate the missing
heirloom."

The young sleuth found sleep impossible. She
kept trying to figure out what Anderson and
Buchanan had been doing. Finally a thought
came to her. "Maybe they had an infrared cam-
era to take pictures, in the dark, of the crooks'
operations as evidence before nabbing them!"

An early-morning phone call from the police
office confirmed Nancy's guess. The men in the
truck had been caught and had confessed to
their part in the sheep racket. The superintendent requested that Nancy and her friends come
to headquarters as soon as possible.

Later at the police office the four girls learned
how Anderson and Buchanan had trailed the
truck. They had taken photographs of the
thieves' every activity, which was irrefutable
proof of their operations.

Mr. Dewar flew into a rage. If the Glasgow
hotel had not made a mistake in the names, he

ranted, and if dumb Paul Petrie had not translated the directions for the sheep smuggling into
Gaelic to impress his boss, the scheme might
have gone on successfully. He had slipped into
Dewar's room and put the note in a bureau
drawer when a chambermaid left the door unlocked while she went down the hall to the linen
closet for clean towels.

"As for you, Miss Drew," Dewar rasped,
"Petrie was supposed to keep you away from
Inverness-shire. He bungled that job too."

Nancy learned that Petrie had caused the
smashup of her car in River Heights, then followed up with the warning note with the piece of
plaid. To scare her further, he had planted the
bomb in the mailbox and telephoned the threat
to Ned. In Scotland he had attempted to force
Nancy's car into a ditch so that she would be
injured and unable to proceed with her
sleuthing.

At this point, Petrie was brought into the
room. The superintendent ordered him to con-
fess his part in the scheme.

The American glared at Nancy. "She's too
smart. Sure, I gave the story about her to the
River Heights *Graphic*. It was to throw suspicion
away from Dewar and me." Petrie suddenly
grinned. "She's smart, oh yes, but I sure gave her
the slip in Edinburgh," he boasted, "when I
used a stolen pass to get into the court building."

Petrie went on to say he took care of the wool and sheepskins which were smuggled by freighter into the United States. Two crewmen had already admitted being involved in the dishonest operation.

"When I found you were coming to Scotland," Petrie said to Nancy, "I thought I'd better get here ahead of you and keep track of your movements. I left a note in Dewar's room to notify him I was here. I suggested the bagpipe signals. You heard me practicing in Dewar's room."

Nancy said, "We figured out most of your Gaelic code message. But we'd like to know the full meaning."

Dewar told her that it indicated the route of the thieves' truck—first a deep ditch to be followed; then a warning to lock the rod on the rear of the covered vehicle carrying the sheep, not merely to close the doors; finally, to transport the wool and sheepskins to the houseboat and to await word about taking the loot to Dumbarton.

Nancy said she had figured out all the sketches on the message except the cradle. "What is the significance of that?"

The prisoners looked at one another, but none answered. Nancy shot a question at them. "Which one of you has a wife who resembles me?"

This time Dewar and Petrie exchanged glances. Finally Petrie shrugged. "I brought my wife over here with me. With a little fixing up, she looks enough like your photograph on the magazine to pass for you. Several years ago she visited Culzean Castle and saw a cradle there in the shape of a boat. When our son was born, she had a cradle made just like it. The sketch was to indicate to Dewar that she was in this country, ready to do her job."

Nancy said she felt very sorry that Petrie's wife had been dragged into the men's dishonest activities. "Then she is the one who was passing the worthless checks and using my name on them? And it was your wife you were phoning in the drugstore to tell her you got my autograph?"

Petrie nodded. He said the words "without stamp" meant that his wife's arm did not bear a certain identifying stamp which the thieves used to identify one another. The forgery scheme was a private deal between Petrie and Dewar.

Nancy and the other girls were praised by the police officer for having solved the mystery. Then Nancy said, "There's someone else who helped us. He's the one who uncovered Paul Petrie's identity in River Heights."

Bess chuckled. "His name is Ned Nickerson."

"Congratulate him for me," said the officer. Turning to Nancy, he asked, "Have you any more questions you would like to ask these prisoners?"

"Yes. I believe Mr. Petrie and perhaps some of his partners know the whereabouts of a valuable brooch which disappeared from my great-grandmother's home."

After considerable prodding, Dewar answered the question. "Lady Douglas' maid, Morag, told a friend that her mistress was going to give the topaz-and-diamond brooch to Miss Drew. I heard the story from this friend and decided it would be a profitable sideline for Petrie and me to steal the pin and divide the money we got for it."

"Where is the brooch now?" Nancy persisted.

"At the bottom of the pond on Lady Douglas' estate!" was the startling reply.

Dewar admitted that he had gone to the house to try to steal the brooch. A dog had barked and almost bitten him. "I had my knockout spray gun with me," he continued. "I gave the dog too much and he died."

Dewar went on to say that just at this point Lady Douglas had come out for a stroll and he had seen the pin on her dress. As he was trying to decide how to get it, the pin had dropped off.

"I waited until she entered the house, and then picked up the brooch. I heard a man's voice and started to run. Suddenly I stumbled and fell. The brooch flew from my hand into the water. I went back one night to try to get the pin from the pond, but two servants were strolling around and I had to give up the idea. Petrie and I decided to try again as soon as you girls left Scotland."

The news electrified all the girls. They could hardly wait to leave headquarters and return to Douglas House. As they rushed in, their cheeks rosy and their eyes shining, Nancy's great-grandmother asked what had happened. Upon hearing the latest information, she too became excited, and as soon as the girls had changed into swim suits, followed them outside, and across to the pond. Morag and Tweedie went along.

The four girls made dive after dive, swimming underwater and searching the leaf-strewn bottom of the pond. On Nancy's sixth time down, she saw something shiny and quickly pushed aside the underwater debris from the object.

It was indeed the topaz-and-diamond brooch!

She triumphantly swam to the surface and waved the pin in her hand.

"You have found it!" Lady Douglas cried out ecstatically. "Oh, Nancy, you have really earned this heirloom—and in a very hard way!"

"But, Great-Grandmother dear, this pin is so gorgeous, it's worth all the effort."

Nancy had decided to refrain from mentioning that Morag had told the story of the brooch to a friend. There seemed no point in upsetting anyone during these happy moments.

Lady Douglas, walking with Nancy back to the

house, suddenly chuckled. "In all the excitement I forgot to tell you some very good news. Your father will be here in time for tea."

"Oh, wonderful!" said Nancy. "He can join in our celebration."

That afternoon the girls decided to dress for the festivities. When Nancy was ready, she made an overseas call to Ned. As soon as he answered, she said excitedly, "The mystery is solved!" She gave a brief account and ended with, "Now I'll have to go and give that little boy, Johnny Barto, an autograph."

"Sure thing," said Ned. "And listen! Don't you dare find another mystery until the June fraternity dance is over!"

"I promise."

After Nancy had hung up, she told Fiona she was going into Bess and George's room. The cousins were not ready, so Nancy sat down in a chair to wait for them.

For a few minutes Nancy was silent, wondering what mystery might come her way next. She was to find out soon, when challenged by *The Phantom of Pine Hill*.

Presently she looked at Bess and said, "I have a confession to make. When I first learned that you had put my photograph in the contest and won, I admit I was worried because of the publicity. But now I want to tell you that your idea turned out to be a very good one."

"Really?" said Bess.

"Yes," Nancy replied, smiling. "Your surprise was a wonderful help to me in finding the clue of the whistling bagpipes!"